Every Good Boy Does Fine

Every Good Boy Does Fine

A Novel by

Tim Laskowski

SOUTHERN METHODIST UNIVERSITY PRESS Dallas

This novel is a work of fiction. Names, characters, places, and incidents are either the product of the author's imagination or are used fictitiously.

First edition, 2003

Cover illustration by Jennifer Hart/*Fort Worth Star-Telegram*

Jacket and text design by Rich Hendel

Library of Congress Cataloging-in-Publication Data
Laskowski, Tim, 1957–
Every good boy does fine : a novel / by Tim Laskowski.— 1st ed.
p. cm.
ISBN 0-87074-477-1 (alk. paper)
1. Brain—Wounds and injuries—Patients—Fiction.
2. Group homes—Fiction. 3. Montana—Fiction. I. Title.
PS3612.A855E95 2003
813'.6—dc21 2003040726

Printed in the United States of America on acid-free paper

10 9 8 7 6 5 4 3 2

This novel is lovingly and respectfully dedicated to some of the most inspiring writers I have known: Dan Lavelle, Devin Walter, Patrick Thompson, Shirley Pendleton, and all those other people with injuries who have helped me understand life a little better, all people of remarkable abilities.

Acknowledgments

Thanks to those who took the time to read my manuscript and offered criticism and encouragement: David Cates, Bryan DiSalvatore, Deirdre McNamer, William Kittredge, James Welch, Allan Bergman, Dr. Nathan Zasler, Michael Valentino, Sheila Thompson, Brenda Toner, Heather Jeanes Holmes, Ted Heuchling, Karin Schalm, and Dr. Thomas Walz. Thanks to Bev Beck Glueckert and Lisa Hofman, who offered artistic expertise. Thanks to Kathryn Lang, who has had faith in my writing and has helped me produce a better novel. Thanks to Angelika Mitchell for her helpful criticism, assistance with the practical chores of getting the manuscript typed and re-typed, and for a love that offers me new beginnings. Thanks to old and new friends and special thanks to my parents, Ray and Clare Laskowski, and to my son, Evan, who has lived with me through it all.

Parts of this book have appeared in *The Ragged Edge* (1997), *Surviving the Western State of Mind* (1999) and the *Brain Injury Association of Montana Newsletter* (Spring 2003).

I imagine myself falling

from great heights—towers or cliffs:

the break of air as I reel,

dead legs spread-eagled in waitless freedom

dark arms splayed and silhouetted

on clouds, head back, long hair afloat,

ears gorged with wind. There in air

before my hard return

to earth, I am not

disabled.

I

At the peak of my piano-playing—right-handed mostly (my left is a gnarled spastic lump I have tried for years to bang out straight on tables and countertops)—my mind empties to allow unsummoned images to flit across the blank screen in my head in no discernible pattern except that the first images are often archways or antique stone facades tumbling into rubble and dust, as in comedy newsreels I've seen where buildings are imploded, collapsing into themselves, so neatly, with the mess contained inside the rock walls of their original foundations. After that, any picture may come: sometimes it is simply myself standing upright, or maybe I am barechested in shorts bounding on a cinder track over aluminum hurdles, or it may be angels lifting my sorry body over curbs and stairs, or it could be animals—wildcat or whitetail deer—leaping brush, twisting in mid-jump, eyes caught in a backwards stare, bleating wonderment as a hunter's bullet singes fur and skin. For me prayer is never an ascension, since I start at the heights and then tumble, the displacement of breath inside me palpable as I spill slow motion from spiritual precipices to the rocky nasty earth where I am again weighted, anchored, no good.

The effort of that first paragraph has been immense—days it has taken to refine—and Ellen bids me to relax. I am head-injured and my cognitive functions are slow to respond, slow to make connections. What's worse, tomorrow I won't recognize the words as mine, unless I now review them over and over and can lock in memory a snatch or phrase to trigger a remembrance from my healthy past (my long-term memory remains relatively sound—a mixed blessing that allows me bittersweet lounging in memories of when I was whole).

There is a past which I remember better than yesterday, when I was healthy, my bones reliable, my muscles responsive to my brain, when my left hand harmonized with my right, when my fingers could flex and drift effortlessly along a keyboard. In my "real life," as my mother has affectionately termed it, I could play the piano, climb a mountain, read philosophy, hold a job, hold a thought longer than a minute. My dreams sometimes linger in that past life. Denial at times becomes remarkably simple for the wheelchair-bound, memory for the head-injured less of a burden than for most.

But in more lucid moments, I struggle against my mother's fantasies, her insistence I will one day return undamaged, the way I had been. Why, after so long, do I still allow my expectant heart to open to her ramblings? Why am I still entranced and fooled by her descriptions of a life that is past? I look around me; I look in the mirror. I must appreciate this, my real life.

I am slow and I repeat. I cannot speak a sentence without it getting tangled on my lips, though inside I hear the words as plain as you might say them yourself. I've come to understand my own speech when I hear it on tape, but others would understand me only with difficulty, with perplexed and guilty study of my face and the few signs I've learned. And Lord, I forget what I say, day to day, hour to hour. Only with many repetitions do I get a routine down. I rely on habit, on stock responses, to fool the able-minded into thinking I understand more than I do. Ellen says it makes no difference if I repeat here, if I stutter on the page. It takes so goddamned long for my head to get the message to my hand to type. The beauty of writing, she says, unlike the spoken word which once said hangs irretrievably in the air, is the ability to revise before it goes public, till you are satisfied your text is indelibly right. Conversation is too quick for me to process. Writing allows me reflection to form the words. For now, Ellen urges me merely to write on.

I have frequent moments of nothing-to-do, when the effort to keep up with the world becomes simply too much, the pace literally dizzying, as in a group session or in dialogue, and my ears shut down, my eyes glaze. I try to reduce input to manageable proportions, and amidst staff shouting and peers' grunts and groans, my mind wanders into meditation, my eyes often focused on the tight grip of my left hand, my fingertips white with strain, cuticles rimmed in red, and an inner voice—desperate for things to slow down—speaks calmly and soothes me. "Robert, Robert," I hear, the name that follows from my premorbid life, delivered sometimes in maternal strains, sometimes in deeper, more masculine tones, sometimes by the voice of staff who try to shake me back to whatever activity I've withdrawn from. Mostly it is comforting—these scrambled waves of messages from my brain—reassuring me that I am, though altered, still lurking in this broken body. If left alone long enough, I can retreat into the voice, sail with the images that flood through me, to a silence where I feel no confusion and no pain.

Usually Ellen waits till the next day to read what I write, though intermittently, she peeks over my shoulder and, in the midst of filling my ears with praise and surprise, cannot resist reaching occasionally to fix the typos and spelling and more obvious grammar errors. I suffer her sighs, her struggle to restrain herself further from my delete key. The story must be mine own, she says, and I remember her saying it more than once, as she sets messages in my brain like newsprint, hoping they remain for a lifetime, or at least a day. It's important I say it uncensored, though she gives suggestions on what to add, what to erase, what to say better. I am, where I am, at the mercy of her criticism. I must grant she is always right, though I refuse her advice at times, usually spontaneously and for no better reason than that the occasional refusal preserves the few boundaries I have left.

Ellen volunteers twice a week at the day program here in Missoula, Montana. I asked for a piano teacher and they found me a poet. I have snuck peeks at her poetry, and these are lines I've forced myself to memorize:

> When the tree falls we hear
> no matter the thickness of the forest
> the muffling of the leaves

The others who started with her have drifted away and I remain her one, her favorite, pupil.

She is older, in her fifties, I guess.

"I had a life once," she says, "with husband and kids. They're all gone now." I worry she depends too much on me, that I am some odd project, some substitute son for her other lost life. I spy her hand wishing for my delete key as she argues this interpretation. "It's too bleak," she whispers, "like I want pity," and of course, she is right, always right, though for now, I respectfully refuse to revise.

She tells me I should explain. Though brain-injured, I am not wholly without powers. A doctor once said my brain knows what to do, and my muscles could follow through, but the messages get blocked somewhere along the way. When my brain says, "Hand open up," or "Lips, make a sound," the signal gets detoured or fails to make a leap between nerve endings, so my acts remain incomplete. In the evenings in the group home, I can stand for an hour at a time, though my attempts to walk result in falling, often taking with me one or more of those hired to care for me. In my wheelchair, I propel myself by pushing with my right foot, while my left stays anchored on a footrest. I wear a strap across my chest to keep me sitting upright, but my head lists steadily to the left. With minimal assistance, I can dress myself in pullover shirts, sweatpants, and shoes with Velcro straps. If a bathroom is well equipped with bars in the right places, I can do my business there alone. Saliva I forget to swallow might pool in the back of my mouth and muffle my speech worse than usual, and the spit drools out a corner of my lips, and I am either wiped or it drips to my lap. I have one good hand, but my left constricts, gnarled, always closed till I or someone else pries the fingers apart and back to clean between them. I am told it tends to smell inside my hand, though I am immune to the odor (and the doctors say I have not lost any sense of smell). For hygiene's sake, they operated on my hand not long ago, relieving a tight tendon, allowing the hand more flexibility. With therapy, I might be able to open it at will, though slowly, to grab a sponge ball or hold a pencil with the proper fingers. The doctors discourage the hope, but I have notions to reach the left side of the keyboard.

I am twenty-three and have been for years, since the fall. I am not always aware time has progressed. On visits, my parents talk of how they've aged and how they plan for me after they're gone, and my sister and brother look older sometimes, though I don't see them often enough to remember them as they are now. I have a son born after my injury, thus a mystery to me since I have no long-term memory of him. In the mirror, I am the same. The scars on my face have long since faded, and I don't believe my appearance has changed for ten years except that my lip corners droop and my glasses are always bent and crooked. So maybe I have grown different—but not older. Even when I become upset about my appearance, my lack of short-term memory benefits me: I soon forget what I'm upset about. I can lose myself anywhere I want in time and place, though there are places I avoid, even in thought, like the hospital and nursing home.

Ah, Ellen sighs. She prods me to introduce things of my life before the accident, but what value is there in that? I was "normal" before I fell, naively undecided in life, just graduated from the University of Montana as a music major, a mystery to those older, those anxious for me to find my way into the workaday world. My accident proved the folly of their plans, their preparations. If I am anything unique now, it is within my present handicap. Only God's select few have my privilege. And Ellen agrees, yes, but she wants to know about the moment when I realized I was not what I had been. She views my flashes of comprehension as brilliance of insight, like an epileptic's aura before the seizure. Yes, she knows my struggle for cognition is fitful and hard. My memory fades in and out like reception on a car radio in mountain ranges. Still, Ellen would suck my frustrations and horrors out onto paper for her enjoyment, not trusting there are aspects of my experiences I can't or won't piece together.

I break my writing often. I have only so much concentration. This will take months, years Ellen says; then I can turn around and revise. She sees this as a lifetime project. I try to beg out: is revision not censoring, a writing over, altering history instead of recording it? A man without memory lives unawares in constant revision of past perceptions.

I have tried hard to understand all the people in my life, but I fail to know who everyone is and what they do. There is, of course, staff: able-bodied do-gooders who get paid very little to feed me, clean me, take me for a dump. They are everywhere, every time. I have few boundaries left. I live with seven other folks like me. Weekdays we come here to this converted warehouse with large community rooms of folding chairs and long tables, where the computers and piano are, where they daily teach us current events and children's games and sometimes a special class or two in photography or computers or writing. Therapists and case managers and a guy from the state come see me. I stopped worrying about identities long ago. I go where and when I'm told. I talk to whoever asks. There seems little difference in my life before or after these people appear.

Many of the others I live with are head-injured like me. A few walk but haven't brain enough left to tell them when to shit or even how to get to the bathroom. I think mentally I do better than most. Then there is Lorna, who has multiple sclerosis, her body shutting down its functions one by one. She lives down the hall from me. We play cards together in the evenings, and I spoon-feed her lunches and dinners. I imagine she was a great beauty once: her hair long brown with a blonde sheen in sunlight and her skin tan and soft as worn velvet. I imagine she took long strolls through lodge pole pines, her bare feet barely disturbing the rust-colored needles of the forest floor, her presence so slight birds did not interrupt their singing on her arrival, animals did not stir and run away as she passed. She had a husband, who has long since deserted her, and two children who live with her parents. Both children and parents cry when they visit. Lorna is deteriorating, I've heard staff say, but I choose not to notice.

The other day (was it today—did it happen more than once?), I sit by myself at a long table in a large room with tiled floor and muted green walls. Others wheel and stumble by or sit at other tables, doing jigsaw puzzles and playing games with checkerlike pieces. There is a scuffle or an argument. Two wheelchairs bang at each other, voices rising, till staff rush over, speak in low but firm tones, separate the combatants. And too quickly the battle is forgotten. Each goes a different way, neither through the door they had fought over.

"How are you today, Robert?" my case manager asks. Her name is Jodi, and I've known her a long time. She is tall and wears heels to make herself taller. She is always so well dressed that I wish I'd remember the times she is due to visit, so I would wear something besides my usual sweats, make sure I am cleanly shaved and recently bathed. Maybe if I was prepared for her arrival, I wouldn't lose my breath when she waltzes into my space. She kneels in front of me, steadies herself with a slender hand on my knee as she studies me with assuringly deep brown eyes, sweeps a stray lock of hair behind her ear, and speaks in a pearly smooth voice, compassionately, and only occasionally with condescension. Oh, I have masturbated many times thinking of her. With her questions, she touches my legs, my arms, my face, as though she has a right to, asking what hurts, what skin rash is healed, what is not, how I am eating. Her usual lecture follows for something I do not do right. She touches my knee again as though she doesn't understand the promise such touches inspire. Many times I have wanted to say don't touch me, but I refrain because I, in fact, desire it. In the night when I am alone, I strive for, and occasionally accomplish, her image, as the touches haunt me.

"Robert, you must brush your teeth more often. You can do that."

"Uhhhhh-huh," I tell her. I have long passed being embarrassed with her, with the regular people in my life. I sign words, form some sounds, and she knows my meaning. Or at least close enough. I try to lock my eyes into hers. Despite many failures, I retain a naive belief my eyes can communicate gists of things, if only the other person is attentive. Jodi makes eye contact briefly then looks away. Is she afraid of the lock of eyes? Maybe, I theorize, it is not the eyes' failure to communicate that makes people turn away, but rather their success at doing precisely that.

It is lonely not to connect, to have people like Jodi come in for fifteen-minute one-sided conversations. Each time hope springs that the connection will be meaningful, will endure, but each time disappointment hunkers in the pit of my stomach when I realize the impatience of my companion who suffers the wait for my next intelligible sound, whose mind has raced to other thoughts while waiting for me. What does Jodi think of when she talks to me? As I stutter and struggle, I give her time to plan her dinner, to imagine her children in school, to recall, goddamn her, her husband that morning rising naked from bed on his slow walk to the shower. I wish Jodi would come when I was ready for her. When I might have planned how to respond to her touch.

Ellen does not blush when she reads my words. She assures me nothing I write can shock her, and so far she is right, though there was a time I tried mightily. I have written about fantasies of suicide; I have written rhapsodies about masturbation, some about her, and she has not flinched. It is the artist in her she says, that demands the search, the grisly along with the pure. It is the artist in me, she says, that demands the same. Perhaps.

But I am disorganized. I can't focus. Please Ellen, I give up. Make this coherent.

No, she says.

2

Jimmy is so goddamned funny tonight, telling jokes to himself. If you think I got it bad, let me tell you: nobody understands Jimmy, though sometimes we pretend to. He's lucky because he can walk with a walker, but I wouldn't trade places with him. He's totally unstuck, wandering from one moment to the next without a clue as to what he's done even a minute ago. Of course, then, he doesn't remember any pain.

"Hey Jimmy," I say, "what the hell day is it?"

Of course, Jimmy can't understand me, though he talks pretty good. He says, quite formally and proudly, "Reagan is president," as though he's answering one of the questions they put to you to see how oriented you are . . . as though it matters to any of us who the president is, what day it is, what month it is.

"Ravioli," Jimmy says, answering another imagined question about what he had for dinner. "Ravioli-oooo," he says and laughs like a retard, and dribbles spit down his chin. Sometimes I'm goddamned ashamed to be brain-injured.

"It's Tue-Friday," he says, "Octovember 93rd." He laughs, thinking he's funny. "1492, when Columbus sailed the TV tube." Yeah it's funny. Everybody laughs, staff and even the other brain-injured residents who don't understand a joke about anything, no matter how many times you explain it. We laugh because it seems vaguely appropriate, and being appropriate is what we strive for, what we live for, waiting for cues from an able-body to know whether we should laugh or goddamned cry or sit there and do nothing.

There is no such thing as normal, Ellen butts in to say, something normal people say a lot. I wonder why they're so anxious to deny normalcy, especially when that's the goal of many of us disabled. From where I sit, it's damned plain to see what's normal and what isn't.

One staff person doesn't think Jimmy is all that funny. Jennifer, I believe, has been working here as long as I've been living here, unusual longevity for a caregiver. She speaks softly with Jimmy, tries to calm him down, because now he's getting louder, shouting his nonsense.

"It's not funny anymore," Jennifer says. "Slow down, Jimmy. Take a breath, Jimmy."

"It's not funny!" I yell at him, ashamed that even as I say it, I can't quite stop laughing. I wheel close to him and in between laughs, I shout in his face, begging him to be quiet. Nobody understands, and Jennifer tries to push my chair away. "Shut up, Jesus, Jimmy," I say. I manage to kick out with my good leg and hit his shin. He stops his shouting then. The idiot grin on his face disappears, and he is all anger now as he jumps toward me, fists swinging wildly. Jennifer instantly is between us, and she takes a light blow on her arm that was meant for me. A male staff holds Jimmy and leads him away to another room where he is soon laughing again.

"Please, Robert," Jennifer says, staring down at me, "go to your room."

I comply. I know I was inappropriate. I was not a good boy. I don't mind being on my own for a while, but soon Jennifer comes in to analyze me. Why am I upset? I don't know why. I don't know how to put my thoughts into the labored stutter and groans that are my speech, and my hand can't sign half of what I want to say. All Jennifer seems to hear is when I shout, "Get the hell out."

She is about to go, to leave in exasperation, but she stops at the door, sighs, and eyes me, her face twisting in an apparent search for words.

"Robert," she says, "Remember the Transitions program?"

She will play dirty with me now. It's a new rehab program she's talking about, where a lot of therapists provide training for brain-injured people to help them live more independently. Staff have been reminding me daily for weeks.

"When you do stuff like kick Jimmy, that jeopardizes your going into the program. You've got to show better judgment."

I turn away from her. I want out of the group home; I want my own place, but I'm always turned down. They say I wouldn't be safe without staff twenty-four hours a day. When I don't turn back to her, when I don't reply, I hear Jennifer sigh again—loudly for my benefit. She doesn't slam the door when she leaves, though she shuts it a little harder than she needs to.

So I'm the bad apple tonight.

Soon after, Lorna knocks and wheels herself in. Though she's lost most of her mind, her instincts are good. She positions her chair next to mine, puts an arm around my shoulders and whispers to me, "Okay, definitely okay, Robert." She speaks about her kids, memories she hangs onto, and I wonder why she thinks I might be interested. Of all of us, Lorna has had the most complete life, premorbid, as they say.

"Robert," she repeats and tries to kiss me. We have begun that, you know. Lorna, my first woman in ten years. If only I were stronger, I could lift myself and her to the bed.

But I can't, and we settle for touches and kisses, and ignore staff prying and peeping through keyholes.

"I wish we were young," Lorna whispers.

I don't understand. Am I not still young, just unable?

3

Morning in bed, and as the general rush outside my door begins, I contemplate the idiocies of my existence. There are moans and squeaks of wheels and mumbles in the corridors, as my housemates begin another day. I am a tree crumpling in the forest, soundlessly crashing in a billowing silent wind. Words I cannot grasp fly above and about me. For a long pausing moment I lie in bed alone, and I vaguely dream of Jodi.

I bellow and lift my back from the sheet, grab a bedpost, reach for the always-waiting wheelchair, swing my legs. But I've forgotten to lock the wheels, and as soon as I make contact with the chair, it scoots away. Like groceries tumbling out of a ripped sack, I fall, limbs scattering, and I scrape an elbow, burn my nose on the low, rough carpet, wishing it was all done in silence, so I might have a chance yet to drag myself into the wayward chair before staff arrives, and maybe they won't notice the thin trail of blood that drips from my elbow to the floor. I've used up my allotment, they've said, of bandages and iodine. They'll take cash out of my account money for more supplies.

I'm way too slow. From behind, staff lifts, then dumps me into the steadied chair. I am firmly admonished to ask for help when I transfer. Staff acts pleasant, but her sighs and the edginess in her voice as she rummages through the bathroom medicine cabinet, let me know her frustration, her pained tolerance.

Sometimes what I write here are composite memories: things

that have happened so often and so similarly they finally reside in my memory as one event. Routine, you see, is the goal of the staff for us poor brain-injured. Did something happen this morning or last week or simply many different mornings? Sometimes I'm not sure. Sometimes I have bursts of clarity when I remember exactly, but such moments do not endure.

The bathroom at the end of my hall is my favorite place in the house, the one room where I'm allowed a few minutes of privacy. As long as there are no zippers or buttons involved, I can pull my own pants down. Steel bars are strategically placed so I can grab and swing myself to the toilet seat, though staff insist I not transfer alone. After they help me, they leave me to do my business, though check back frequently so I'm not tempted to try to transfer back to my chair by myself. On bath days, with a minimum of help, I can shift to the edge of the bathtub. I need assistance to settle myself into the water where I am granted a half-hour of uninterrupted soaking time. Unfortunately I need help to wash my hair and to get out and to dry myself.

At breakfast I try to help feed Lorna since her hands have become unresponsive to what she wills for them. I have enough control of my right hand to spoon up her mashed food. Though I'm famous for making a mess of myself when I eat, somehow I can concentrate and be just careful enough with Lorna that I don't shake when I lift the spoon to her mouth. Lately she has had trouble swallowing and so staff hover over us, watching closely the flight of the spoonfuls towards her, usurping my place when I go too fast or too slow or simply when scheduled time grows short, and they urge me to eat my own meal. When feeding myself, I grow tired of concentrating, and I spill or dribble cereal or eggs down my front, onto my lap. Most days, I'm layered with napkins and a bib.

Outside waiting for the van to take us to our day services, I wheel myself close to Lorna so our wheelchairs are touching. We sit hand in hand in the driveway, shaded by the paper birch, whose frail jagged leaves seem to interrupt the sunlight and sparkle with the last remnants of dew. My hand drifts to her thigh and rests there temporarily. I daydream of when I was a boy climbing a young birch, getting so high, then arching its slender top downwards back towards earth. Only so high before the descent begins. My hand stretches no higher than Lorna's bunched sweat pants allow. She stares straight ahead, smiling. "Definitely," she says, her standard response to questions and situations.

"Not here," staff admonishes and separates us. The van arrives. Lorna and I take our turns on the mechanical lift, efficiently upwards and in.

There is assembly work today at the day service: stuffing labels into plastic bags that will eventually hold loaves of bread, but they don't allow me this work due to my drool, and that's okay with me. They pay by the piece for whatever we do, and the last time I worked, I got something like a dollar fifty-four for two weeks. I am bored here.

There is an old piano in the corner, untuned, largely unplayed by anybody except me. In my real life, I still remember the notes: quarter, half, whole. I remember their places on and between the lines: *Every Good Boy Does Fine.* But I can't maintain rhythm. I can't move my fingers swiftly enough, with proper cadence, to capture any melody, even if it's a song I know well, like Christmas carols I've known a lifetime. If someone else is playing, I can almost keep up with the words or hum the tune, but if I'm on my own, on the piano or singing or humming, I can't keep it straight. My mind either lurches ahead or lags behind my abilities.

I hunch over the keyboard, my ear nearly resting on the keys, my eyes nearly level with the long black and white row. I am very deliberate in my playing and watch as my hand hits each key, pausing often, keeping my little finger on one key, trying to use the edge of the adjacent key to open up my hand so my thumb can reach five, six keys down. At times it works, but usually the back of my hand ends up rolling over the keys, disrupting whatever melody I've managed to capture. In "O Holy Night," between notes I need to stretch eight keys from a low G to a high G. I start okay: three E half notes, slight jump to G, then another G, two A's, F, A, C, G. "Long lay the world in sin and error pining . . ." Pine trees are slandered, trees so large and steady and independent. Do they really pine? for what? sun? underground water? Or do they take these for granted? My life is a pining for roots, for balance to stand and reach. Christmas is when God appears but doesn't save and I lose myself in the carols I try to play.

No matter how cracked and disrupted the carols emerge from under my clumsy hands, when I play them, I get lost on a flight of daydreaming, of meditation. I feel airy. I imagine myself a concert pianist with slender fingers that can dance over the keys, fingers with memory more astute than my own, fingers that can trace the way without aid of eyes or mind, that obey the ear, till I am lifted from my seat, hover on air, till I am music without instrument, a capella, without assistive devices, my escape into that weightless vacuum, on a night when gods strive to redeem the heavy heavy earth.

"O night." Then comes the leap between octaves, between G and a higher G, that holy leap from the first syllable to the next in "di—Vine." My fingers scramble, rhythms are crumpled, mangled, and the song sighs, destroyed in the suspension. I am left bent over on my seat, my ear on the keys, my forehead bathed in sweat. By the time I reach the higher G, it's too late. The song is lost. I am left pining.

I think I see Jodi once a week at the day service. It's not always me she comes for, but if I see her, I flag her down, engage her in conversation. Too often she's in a hurry, but once—a year ago or years ago—I remember she took the time. She took me in her car for lunch. I don't remember the occasion—perhaps my birthday, perhaps we were new to each other, and she wanted to find out more about me. She wore a black skirt and black stockings and a black blouse. At least, that's what I now imagine. She ate a salad with ranch dressing. I ate a burger with ketchup and pickles. She studied me as I talked and asked questions about family, my past.

I have a son, I said, and I saw she didn't believe me. His name is John. He lives with his mother. I don't remember exactly where but my parents know. I grew up outside Wolf Brook, a tiny town on Montana's High Line. I've always enjoyed saying High Line, though it's such an aspiration for the small towns on Highway 2. It's called the High Line because the road stretches across the northern part of Montana. East of the Divide, where Wolf Brook is, it's all flat, dry, and windy prairie land. Dust blows into your eyes during the hot summers. In winter, blizzards billow snow into piles along the fences and onto the road. My family has a ranch there, and I play the piano, and at one time I attended the University of Montana, and lived here in Missoula, in the heart of the Montana Rockies, where the mountains provide shelter from the wind and draw the rain so the land is greener and fresher than in eastern Montana. One day near here, I climbed a mountain. I have no memory—not even a glimmer—of how I got down, but I often dream of falling, spinning, twirling in space, awakening in a hospital bed. I was near the top, my friend has told me. It was a long way down.

I don't remember much about my lunch with Jodi, except as a fact that it happened, and I remake it each time I think about it. I like to believe she reaches under the table for my upper thigh, that sometimes we simply laugh, enthralled by each other's wit and sincerity.

I guess I've told her everything important. I know I am written down in her files, the black-and-white papers she keeps folded under her arms.

Pat, spiffy in suit and tie, leans over and spins the brightly lit wheel. The camera pans to three ordinary people standing and looking tense, excited, then to Vanna clapping and a letter board behind her with half a phrase spelled out. "When Johnny Comes Marching Home," Lorna guesses from her bed. I sit in my chair next to her, holding her hand. Together we watch the TV propped on her dresser near the foot of her bed. A large triptych of pictures of her children is set to the side of the TV. I don't think her mother and father know the extent of our relationship, though occasionally they've sat with us at lunch. They know I help feed Lorna. They know I figure somewhere in the equation. Though I can't figure these puzzles on TV, I like to watch Vanna turn and smile, as the letters appear like magic behind her hands. The camera doesn't remain focused long enough for me to even guess at any emergent meanings.

"You get 'When Johnny Comes Marching Home' out of that?" I ask Lorna. I did see a "W" in there, but then I know Lorna never guesses right.

"Definitely," she replies. She used to ask me to repeat myself a lot, but then she learned enough of my speech to know the gist of what I say. Still, our communication is garbled, especially lately since her voice has softened, and at times she slurs.

"Are you seeing your family again soon?" I ask.

"Definitely," she says.

“Your kids are decent,” I say. There’s two girls and a boy, near teenagers or thereabouts. They don’t talk to me other than to mumble embarrassed hellos. Her parents are kinder, ask me questions about how I’m doing, though they don’t wait for my answers.

My parents used to visit often, but it’s a rare occasion now. They still live in Wolf Brook in eastern Montana, five hundred miles from here, and I used to go there a few times a year, though now I go only for Christmas. My dad says he can’t lift me anymore, and my brother is married and not living in the main ranch house. Last Christmas, my son John was there. He’s thirteen or so now, born right before my accident, or right after. I never keep that straight. Anyway he’s not in my long-term memory anywhere, not like my parents, my brother and sister. And Wolf Brook itself. Seeing John is like encountering an alien at home, a bit like the nieces and nephews I can’t keep track of since I don’t see them often enough, and they weren’t there when I first left the real world of Wolf Brook.

I have tried cementing John in my memory. I once carried his baby picture everywhere, studying his face and tiny fingers, repeating like a mantra this was my son, that I was a father, but when I saw him in the flesh again, he was over a year old, and he looked nothing like the picture, so I had no idea who he was. I have not seen him every Christmas, and I’m not sure if his mother is still in Wolf Brook. But I think it was last Christmas I saw him, and he turned away from me, didn’t say more than two words to me, and I don’t blame him. He’s at that age, my sister told me.

Lorna squeezes my hand. I look at her, and she smiles weakly. Invisible people clap and cheer for new letters, a new puzzle. I don’t think Lorna got the last one right. “Come here,” she says and I undo my seat belt, scoot my butt to the front of my wheelchair. She grabs my hand and runs it under her blankets to a bare thigh. With my good right hand, I grasp a bed post, rock myself till I have enough momentum to launch myself out of the wheelchair onto the side of her bed. I teeter off-balance, but my right foot steadies me, and I push so that I am beside her on the bed. I lean and hold her, kiss her cheek, then her mouth. I reach between her legs and try to slip a finger under her panties. There’s equipment blocking the way, and my clumsy hand dislodges it. She throws an arm around my neck and wraps me tight but a warm wet puddle forms beneath us, and she yells. In seconds, staff is there, picking me off the bed, settling me—grunting and sighing—back into my chair, their voices only slightly raised, tinged with annoyance. I am roughly wheeled to the bathroom, and they begin a bath for me.

"You can't do it, Robert," staff says. "We'll have to take Lorna to the hospital to get her catheter replaced. We won't be able to leave you two alone again."

I'm left in peace, alone for a while. In the tub I can keep myself steady, head above the water. I like to soak. Some important things I can force myself to remember, but most things just won't stick. Like with Lorna. I know better than to do what I did, but I forget at crucial moments. A therapist once said I have no judgment skills and little idea of safety—my own or others'—even though my memory is better than others who are brain-injured like me. Well, I soak and I choose to forget. I imagine myself in bed with Jodi, her long limber legs about my neck. If I let the fantasy run amok, I envision myself whole, the man I was in my real life, but sometimes I enjoy imagining myself as I am, with my disabilities, being cared for. Jodi bathes me, attending especially to the most sensitive areas. She enters the tub, eases her healthy body across my broken one. She does all the work while I lean back and enjoy, lost in frenzy. She kisses my face, licks at my ear, presses her breasts across my bare chest.

Fantasies of Jodi end in relief, then regret. The second after they end, Lorna's face haunts me, and guilt overcomes me. But Lorna cannot be for me what Jodi is.

4

I don't remember, except in snatches, I tell Ellen. She says that's fine. Write what I remember. How I write is as revealing as what I write, she says, so concentrate more on style than content. But I want to get it right, to get the facts straight. She doesn't understand this urgency, that everything swirls about me and I hope by writing to fix it, to hold it down, to let me examine this world for a longer time than I can normally. She smiles. Writing is like trying to remember a dream, she says. It's a race to remember events exactly as they happened, knowing that just as time passes in the telling, the dream fades, details lost. I'm not unlike everyone else, she says; just my memories fade faster. She gives me a mini-cassette recorder and suggests I tell my story just as things happen, then together she and I can review the tape and reconstruct the details in writing. This is what I do though often neither one of us can understand much of what I've said on tape. Don't worry so much, she says. Ultimately, all writing is fiction. Writers make up what they think they hear and see. We write our own versions, and that, she stresses, is what she wants from me. My version. It doesn't matter to her that I am not satisfied. I bank my entire existence on finding an anchoring reality, some common touch of the world outside me I can appreciate with others, both abled and disabled. I want consistent patterns, base truths, permanent connecting points. None of us have those, Ellen laughs while I record. Frantically, I tape my impressions as quickly as possible, and sometimes I just let the machine run during an event, a conversation, hoping this little machine can fill in for my memory. It's easy for Ellen to accept no objectivity. She's not threatened daily with being unstuck, cognitively adrift.

I ask Ellen to leave this passage alone, just edit the absolute necessaries after I'm done, and let me reveal, be revealed. If only my fingers could fly over the keys as fast as my thoughts whirl, I'd like for a moment to be known uncensored, though I don't know why or who will do the knowing, and I feel so revealed already. Can there be anyone more on display than a disabled person, worst foot forward, so to speak, and in my case, even my most private habits are known, if not actually studied. Though yes, I fear they are studied. We are creatures of habit, of routine, we brain-injured, and if you discover our routine you may mold us, help us, not rile us, not be embarrassed too much by us. Damn, I go too slow to keep any momentum, any consistency in the story, and what is that, exactly, do you suppose? I was whole once, in college and before, and sometimes I convince myself I actually remember the handhold, the pivot move necessary to reach the next hold, and I reimagine the rope singeing my cheek, and what was next? Some misstep? Some ill wind, some goat perhaps that jostled a pebble, which dislodged a larger stone, some tremor from another side of the mountain, causing my foot to slip? I don't know; I'll never know. For months after the coma I remembered nothing of the day, let alone the hour, or the minutes before or after. Even now in lucid flashes, with what others have told me, I try to re-create remnants of the time. I think one friend was above me, another below me. Then there is only dark, like the tunnel I've heard people speak of at death, and the light appeared after a long sleep, as the white fluorescence of a hospital room, and no one, not a soul around to see me open my eyes, to grunt. Did I feel like an infant just descended from the canal, though with minimally more cognition than my first birth, and more terror, since I would have roughly known I had been here before?

And I feel the tunnel continues, gray now not black. I feel I am in for the long haul . . . thirty years or forty or fifty; I can live as long as anyone. I am susceptible to more accidents, though safety-buckled in this chair, though hardly mobile with little chance to exceed maximum speeds, to be reckless, to take risks. . . . Occasionally the sentence dawns on me and I writhe, I grunt a little louder, I moan the heart of my complaint, like a child. What horrors I present to those who love me.

A noise like a watch ticking and a rustle of clothes. I shut my eyes, and she moves gently behind me, in gray cotton socks, in soft corduroy slacks that swoosh, in silken green blouse and hair flowing like a waterfall down about my face, my eyes, my shoulders, her hands like warm butter melting across me. Then a squeak and groan of a steel wheel. Why do I dream her this way? Lorna was never the way I imagine, as I replace her body, her face, her self with others more attractive, less accessible to me, and I edge my eyes upward, hoping for Ellen to lay a hand across this keyboard, to delete, to edit, to fix, but she is not here. At my request she stays away, and she will not revise, not for now, not this.

"Come on, Robert, Robert, Robert, Robert. This way, Robert." This is how I remember Jodi's voice today. I whisper into my recorder.

I sit in the doctor's waiting room. I have been here before, I'm told, though not often enough to remember. Jodi talks to me, asks about something, checks on something. The carpet is blue with yellow-gold swirls, like a paisley tie. I stare so long the pattern seems to move, and it makes me feel sick. Jodi chatters away, I imagine, about the weather or a matter of no consequence. I don't think she's talking to me anymore—something about water-skiing on Flathead Lake, about her son, her family. If you follow the gold swirl pattern, it looks like an egg yolk just as it's beaten, just beginning to unfold, and I begin to laugh, then remember where I am. Where I am I should be solemn, in the doctor's office where people are sick, where silence is desired, like church, but knowing this makes me laugh harder. Jodi chants, "Robert, Robert, Robert."

"How are you today?" the doctor asks when I'm wheeled into his room. His singsong voice sparks a remembrance in me, and I know I have been here before. This is Doctor So-and-So. He looks at the scars on my inside wrist and palm, feels them, and asks about pain. He gives me a sponge ball to demonstrate my grip. He measures how far my fingers stretch. "Okay," he says. "You're improving."

Jodi gives a report on me. Staff must feed her information since she seems to know about all I do at home and work. I am fine, she says, except I don't wait for help with transferring, and I try to sneak off by myself at times. I am anxious to try the new Transitions rehab program, she says, and then I interrupt to ask what she is talking about. She laughs and tells me that I know, that she's told me all about the new program for brain-injured people at the hospital. The doctor says I can start next week.

She is concerned, Jodi tells the doctor. I have a special woman friend at the group home who is not doing well. They have talked with me, she says, but I don't seem to understand she is so sick, that . . . she hesitates and lets the sentence drop.

Lorna? I ask. Are you talking about Lorna? When have you talked with me about her? I don't remember.

There is this advantage these folks have over me, always able to say I've been told, I've been informed, and if I don't remember, the fault is mine.

We will, I tell the doctor, take Lorna shopping tomorrow. We will cruise the mall. Tomorrow I will do that.

I turn quickly enough to see Jodi shaking her head, canceling my plans.

5

I go to church and sing to Jesus, the flower of my voice droning and husky, racing after the melody, occasionally slipping into harmony with the congregation. I love church, the press of well-dressed crowds, people smiling in sympathy, pausing for a few moments to ask about me, to shake my hand, the pastor meeting me at the door, never failing to remember my name, and young women looking with concern at me. I don't go every Sunday, but I go often enough. During the pastor's homily, I pray, and allow myself to drift in dreams, secrets wandering into my consciousness, images of hands reaching for my body, lifting me like a Host, and a host of sinners surround me, the mystery in the center. I am so often weightless in my prayers, though I don't pray for it, don't pray for cures, for miracles. I just shut down my mind as best I can and let my weightless soul float through images, hoping for the day's revelation. If a priest could just lift me high so I could have unobstructed views of my surroundings—why I could see my home from here, as the old joke goes, a joke that pre-dates my injury, rattles around my head like loose change.

I'm afraid of these clichés, afraid my prayers are just rehashes of nothing profound, nothing of insight. I'm covering old ground over and over, and . . .

I went to church last Sunday with my family. My parents were in town with my son, John, one sock off and one sock on. It's spring and the scents of growth penetrate everywhere. Everywhere is that new green, green, green that comes only at the beginning of spring, and the smells are wet and blossoming inside your head, billowing in the cavities behind the nose, between the ears.

The snows have melted on the High Line. You know how hard it is to travel in winter. My parents always apologize for not coming more often and spout vain promises of visiting more when the weather's fine. But I rarely miss them and they don't believe me when I say I have no wish to live with them anymore, that I prefer being where I am, I have my life here now. Sometimes my mother sidles up to me and whispers how sorry she is they couldn't keep me at home, and how they've always planned to retrieve me one day, but now they're getting older and Dad's back isn't what it used to be. There are times I wish I lived with them just so they'd get used to me as I am.

We walked after church on the blacktopped path along the river, my father pushing me, my mother alongside, and John lingering behind, sullen, forced here on this trip by my parents and maybe by his own guilt. Last Christmas, I wished not to see him again unless he wanted, and I tried to say that, but I guess things were miscommunicated. I understand, I want to say. Maybe we'll have our time together, but now I'm an embarrassment and a thing to be feared by a boy his age. I have time. I will wait.

It's not as though I know him anyway. He is not in my long-term memory. He grows and is vastly different every time I see him. I can't fix any image of him in my brain. I don't remember any ways of how to relate to him, how to connect, and he is one of the only people in the world who make me profoundly uncomfortable. Nobody else expects anything more from me than what I can give except him. He's always watching, wanting more than I do myself for me to get up, to walk, to approach normalcy.

Today the grass is lush green in the brief temporary pause of Montana spring, between the decaying muddy snow and the summer-dried brown. It is never green for long. The path is a blacktopped snake slicing through grass and occasional small trees. Behind a low concrete wall is the river and its embankments of sand and driftwood and weeds and hidden nests. I used to know something of wild things. The path winds around two old chestnut trees. In the last days of summer, the spiky shells will crackle under my wheels, though now the trees sigh in blossoms.

My mom chatters about the weather, then how she prefers it here in western Montana and the mountains to the flat cold plain where they live. But Missoula is too big, the traffic too much, the people too hurried.

"Someday we'll take you home for good," she chatters. "When you're better. It'll be back to your real life then."

Her babbling doesn't irritate me like it used to, and we both ignore my dad's frowns and sighs. Though I know better, sometimes I allow myself to be wrapped in her delusions, to be carried away with visions of an able life.

"This new rehab program might be just the ticket," she says, "to get you up and walking again, and goodness knows what else."

"The social worker says don't expect no such thing," Dad says, always the bitter realist. "Why do you go on so? You just make things worse."

Occasionally I love to luxuriate in their bickering. It stirs up old memories of home that have not yet faded.

"Well, who knows, once they start giving him the therapy he needs. I always said it was just a matter of the right therapy, the right people doing the right things. Robert was always so quick to learn. Nobody ever gave him a chance. And look at the operation on his hand. Already he can open it an inch more, I bet. They're just beginning with all their new technology. Why are men always so gloomy? Not Robert, of course. He's never given up, right honey? You've never given up. We'll be back to real life soon."

"There ain't no miracles," Dad says, and I know he's right, even as I listen to the possibilities flush from my mother's heart.

Mom and Dad rest on a bench by a display of three giant carved metal trout, statues among rocks, in poses of searching. John has inherited pushing me, and I signal him to come around to my side. If he doesn't mind slowing down, I can propel myself with my hand on a wheel and my right foot stepping in front of me. I wish I could remember his age. I know he's past ten, and if I struggle hard enough, I might come up with a number. God knows, I might be the father of a teenager by now, so, despite my forgetful denials, I am getting old. He is so serious that I laugh, then swear because I feel I am the child here, so nervous and unsure, wanting desperately to be appropriate. I never want to be normal more than when I am with him. He is kinder today than I remember, more patient. His fine dark hair is two-tiered, very short above his ears, then flopping messily from the upper layer. He is scrawny in untied, high-top sneakers and baggy pants and an oversized T-shirt. Is he my spitting image? Did I look like him once? Pray to God he will never be crumpled like me now. I am sure I am a burden for him, and I wonder if I provide some lesson as well, at least some cautionary example of what can go wrong if you are not always careful.

"John," I say, and he studies my lips with exaggerated seriousness. He recognizes his name. "I love you, John. I'm happy you visit."

"Okay, Robert," he says. I don't ever recall being "Dad" to him. "Gramma says you always ask about me. She gives me the cards and gifts you send."

I don't remember sending anything, but who can tell? I don't argue with him.

"How's your mother?" I ask. Try as I might, I can't recall her name.

"Okay, Robert," John says, and I know he doesn't understand me. I swallow and sit up straight and try again, as slow and clear as I can:

"YOUR MOTHER?"

"Oh," he says. "She's fine, still working in the bakery. She asks about you, you know."

I look past him to my parents among the metal trout.

"John, do you like to go fishing?"

He asks me to repeat, and he concentrates harder on my face as I try again. Again he asks me to repeat, and after the third time, he just smiles.

"Okay, yeah, Robert, right."

I signal with my good hand, but he doesn't know sign language, and we are left studying each other. I grab his hand and try to pull him into a hug with me but he resists, holds back, and I slump in my chair, left looking at the chestnut trees, the concrete wall behind them, glimpses of river water beyond.

"Okay," I say and let thoughts and words fly uncontrollably. "Fishing," I say, and cast an imaginary line towards the river. "DO YOU FISH? John, I wish you lived here so you could take me fishing. I tried going but, what happened? I couldn't bait the hook or something. I couldn't cast worth a damn. I used to fish pretty good when I was a kid. Flies and bait. Trout everywhere, I remember, streams so full you could walk across on their backs—or was that just my dad's story about when he was young? Does it matter whose memories I have? They're just stories, Ellen would say, fictions of what used to be. I'm writing a book, you know, and I write poetry. Let me show you."

I know he hasn't followed this speech, so I try to reach the backpack that hangs behind my chair. John is quick to help and produces the binder that holds the poetry I've typed on the day program's computer. I hand the binder to him and signal him to read.

He sits on the grass, opens the binder, then delivers a scrunched-up face, and I remember most of what I have is unedited, untouched yet by Ellen, and the misspellings, typos, non sequiturs, and needless repetitions haunt the pages yet. I look over his shoulder:

fish in hte park
they are browen cast medal
fixed in realistic poses
for a walk-by audyence
of siteseers and toristas
the reel fishermen,
who no the whirls and swirls
of rivers, of eddies in and out,
are not fooled
but pawse anyweigh
for memorys cast in metal

"I'm better than that," I try to explain. "These are just drafts." I try to pull the binder away, hope to find a more finished piece, but John holds the book back and reads on, till he finally stops and looks at me.

"You wrote this stuff?" he asks, squinting at me, sunlight shining from behind me.

He closes the binder as carefully as I've seen anyone, rises and places it slowly and solemnly behind me and begins to push me.

"I didn't know, Robert," he says. "I never understand you when you talk. I never know what's inside you. I'm sorry."

He pushes me to my parents, who stand now, waiting for us. It's getting dark and they need to head home to the High Line.

6

If I could, I would write fiction all day and poetry by night, but it's such a labor, and not just physical. I can't quite string the stories together, make them linger into coherence, as the ideas break down too rapidly, disperse even before the words form on the screen. My head won't stay set straight forward. Truth should be a little easier. I don't have to worry about plot lines or lies gone awry if I just write my day, what I remember, what Ellen helps to reconstruct. She fidgets, wondering when we'll meet again now that I am about to embark on the new Transitions rehab program: no more day services for me. Jodi says Ellen can be written into my new schedule, if the Transitions staff don't mind.

Ellen is all over these words, shaping them, violating them, so I wonder how much of the story is mine. What if I were uncensored? What if the words were presented as I originally write them? Am I too garbled, too much a mistake to be let loose?

Even the best writers have editors, says Ellen, who's always ready with an answer. But temporarily, let us descend, I argue, to my level:

> Beuty of the daye oer me lies like wisper of a woman I once new Poetry jaggs in my head from all angels, from all angles, I repeat Todaye is the daye I start a new programm at the hosspital Thats what someone reminded me that Jodi comes to take me todaye.

Loorna looks at me and holds my hand and I fele vagely guilty that Im leving her, at least not ackompaning her to the reglar daye service, i dont think she knowse the detales that I wont be there for luntch to help fede her or sit outsyde a wile in the warm sun. she holds my hand and stars at my face, knowse that much that something is diffrent todaye, something is changing She smiles and wishes me, "luck, defnitely luck," she says She has the instinks of an angle Defnitly.

I think of are times, of a nite in bed, holding close, kissing, my hand delving uphigh, her legs buckling besyde me. What nites, what misterys we shared while even then I contimplayted my myseries, my inabilitys to preform more adeptly, these hands of mine that I remember once playing Chopin simphonies and I wuld replay those meldodys in my mind in times when I once grabbed rock on rock up a mountin slope, up thru clowds about my head.

And downward down to a realitie till Jodi appeers, a viszion of blond hair caskading, kneeling in front of me, asking if Im reddy for a trip to where they might put me back together She reprisents my dreems, my prayres, for her I will goe to the very jaws of normalsy.

I leeve with not much more than a nodd to Loorna and those staph congrating behynd her.

Ellen restrains no more. She attacks the delete and edit keys with a vengeance worthy of an editor scorned. We will leave that patch of words above for a reader's glimpse into the difficulty of her task, she laughs, though she promises to be more selective, to restrict her editings to misspellings, obvious contradictions, needless repetitions, confusing syntax. She will be more ghost and less writer.

In the car I can't help but watch Jodi's stockinged legs glisten in the filtering sunlight, one ankle bent for the accelerator. I don't understand why she's the one woman I can't let go of, the one woman I obsess over, the one I do not forget. Though I don't see her that often, my memory is sound when I recall her image. She's been too friendly, too free with her smiles and touches.

"Robert," she smiles, "the first thing they'll do at the new program is just talk with you, ask you a million questions, get to know you and figure out what you want, what they might help with."

"My hand," I say. "I want to play the piano. And I want to live in an apartment. By myself."

She's focused on the road, not looking at me, so she doesn't understand what I'm saying.

"No miracles," she says. "I don't want to give you false hopes. We want to expand your independence, but most things will remain the same for you."

We pull into a long driveway leading into a large parking lot filled with cars on display before tremendous brick buildings: the hospital. I feel twinges of despair and fright. I remember hospitals as darkly white, ghostly halls of chambers where they prick and pry at you and experiment on your brain. I've been to this hospital before, off and on, Jodi tells me. Her office is in an outbuilding near the new rehab program. I might see her daily, and that cheers me up, makes me less frightened.

Jodi sits next to me. Two workers from the group home are here, too. The rest are new to me. They gather around like long-toothed wolves, and I a weak straggler from the herd. Bumbling over themselves trying to be friendly, therapists with that sickly sweet tone of voice I cringe at, the voice of pity and veiled disgust. They're talking to me, and I switch on my tape recorder for their introductions, and I try to stay focused, try to follow their words, but my mind busts loose occasionally. One sits in the corner in a striped green shirt, like a football field newly chalked for the big game on Friday night. Images emerge of a girl—Mary Lou? Under the bleachers, we laughed and fondled and wrestled with each other till the rafters shook as the crowd stomped and roared for the home team.

"Robert, what are your goals?" a woman asks and stares intently. I force myself to focus.

"My hand," I say. It's become a rote answer. "I want to play the piano like I used to. I want to be able to stretch to reach the keys. I want my brain to flow more smoothly over the music. I want . . ."

"Slower, Robert," the woman smiles. "Please sit up straight, take a breath, swallow, and speak slower." I do what she says. She gives me full attention as I repeat, calmly.

"He's mostly recovered from the surgery on his hand," Jodi says. "He's been doing daily exercises, and the doctor feels he's probably near maximum flexibility now."

"Robert," the woman says. Her name is Clare, and I figure she's the boss. She kneels next to me, holds my left hand in hers, and gradually plies the fingers one by one, stretching them full-length, then tracing the white scar that runs from wrist to mid-palm. When she is done, my hand shrivels shut again, a spastic lump.

"We can't promise big changes," she says, "but we can help with some things. I understand you'd like to move into your own place, and we need to identify what your barriers are."

With colored markers on a white board on the wall, she creates columns. One of the columns lists goals. Most are mine. Some are coaxed from me; some are what they say I want. This is their list. As Ellen feeds it verbatim into the computer, she tsks tsks about the reduction of people into formulations:

GOALS
1) Speak more clearly
2) Improve use of left hand
3) Eat safely
4) Move to an apartment, with roommate and staff assistance
5) Work or volunteer
6) Play the piano better
7) Walk with walker
8) Use electric wheelchair
9) Improve transfers
10) Eliminate sexual inappropriateness
11) Increase attention to appearance and hygiene
12) Increase physical endurance

Then barriers:

Cognitive:
1) Impaired judgment/safety
2) Inconsistent planning

3) Inconsistent use of compensatory strategies
4) Short-term memory deficits

Physical:
1) Fatigue
2) Limited physical control, especially left side
3) Drooling

Self-management:
1) Limited awareness of others' needs
2) Limited knowledge of home management skills
3) Poor hygiene, appearance

Then strengths, which Jodi and the group home staff spill out:

1) Likes people/sociable
2) Motivated to improve
3) Polite/good manners
4) Hard worker
5) Likeable
6) Infectious laugh
7) Writes poetry
8) Plays piano
9) Listens to radio
10) Open-minded
11) Accepts feedback well
12) Sense of humor
13) Positive attitude
14) Sense of community/belonging
15) Good-looking
16) Great mustache

It is accomplished. I can start tomorrow.

7

Mornings here begin with a gathering of patients and therapists. Staff greet each other and us with jokes and small talk, then review our plans for the day; that is, we patients review the staff's plans for us. Not a bad arrangement since then I don't need to think much. A week after I've started and I am never left alone. Always someone is trailing me with questions or directions. "Sit straight. Swallow before you speak." Or we play games, like Connect Four, and we put together jigsaw puzzles, testing my memory, my cognitive skills. I talked once with a psychologist, and he will do some testing of me.

Brett is a staff here, in charge of my day. He watches me with intense eyes, says I'm being evaluated. They're seeing what they have to work with, where I need help, where help is possible. In the kitchen, Brett tells me to make my lunch. I shuffle through the refrigerator for the bologna but then can't get the damn package open. "We can devise packages that are easy for you to open," he says and pulls out two pieces, places them on a plate. "What next?" he asks. The question throws me. What next? I can't focus on its meaning, and I panic searching for the right answer. What next? Goddamn it. I crumple up the bologna in my right hand and look at Brett. He grabs my hand, asks me to release the bologna. "Bread," he whispers. "Robert, you need bread." I feel so dumb I want to crawl away. I look around the small kitchen, vainly trying to discover the bread. "Here," Brett says, pointing to the loaf, wrapped in a plastic bag, right in front of me on the counter. "Damn," I mutter. "Relax," says Brett.

I take a deep breath. I steady the loaf with my clumsy left hand, crushing the bread a bit, and with my right, I untwist the tie. It takes me a while, but I'm successful. I pull the bag into my lap and reach for a couple slices. But I end up crunching the loaf, squeezing it between my arm and chest. I've been concentrating so much on what my hands are doing I don't notice till too late that a silvery line of drool dangles and falls into the open bag. Brett reaches for the bread but I quickly throw the bag across the kitchen. "Damn," I say.

"Okay, Robert," Brett says. "It's your first time. It takes repetition to get these things down right."

I have two gnarled pieces of bread in my right hand. I set them on a plate and try to smooth them out. Gingerly, I place the bologna on the bread. I take my time, real slow, till I've made the sandwich.

"Mayonnaise," Brett says. "Did you forget the mayonnaise?"

Of course, I think. Yes, I've forgotten the damn mayonnaise, but I won't admit another failure. Instead I stammer "No" to Brett. "Never use mayonnaise." The words are hard to spit out, in the midst of trying to chew the driest, most mangled sandwich I've ever had. The food sticks to the roof of my mouth, and when I try to say more, I cough and spit out pieces of bologna and bread onto him. I wheel back, away from Brett, who first looks surprised, but then his face breaks into a grin, and he laughs. "You sure about no mayonnaise, Robert?"

He grabs the mushy sandwich from my grip, opens it up on the counter, and spreads on it liberal amounts of mayonnaise.

Brett is right. A few tasks get easier with repetition, but still staff remind me constantly of even the smallest things. I have trouble remembering sequences, trouble staying focused on what I'm doing. Especially by the afternoon, I get tired out, and they've recommended naps for me, but it makes me feel too much like a child.

Brett takes me to a piano in a large recreation room in the hospital. He says he wants to hear me play.

"I haven't played for a while," I say.

"Come on, Ludwig. Let's hear you."

He moves the piano bench away so I can wheel to the keys, and he sits on an overstuffed couch, next to the piano. It has been two weeks since I've started Transitions, two weeks since I've sat in front of a piano, and I can't remember any audience before.

"Did you ever hear a mazurka?" I ask. "I was a good piano player. Back in my real life." I want to explain to Brett what I used to know about the odd spirited melancholy in Chopin's mazurkas, but he interrupts. He grabs my left hand and stares intently at me. "This is your real life," he says.

I place my right hand on the keys, thumb on middle C. I lay my head sideways, just above the keys, my gaze skimming the tops of them. I carefully pick out the first few notes of "Silent Night," then slowly lift my left hand up for the chords. A white scar links my wrist and palm, a bright jagged line against the redness of my hand. You can still trace where the stitches have been. I pause the melody to pry the fingers of my left hand apart as much as possible. The hand can open more than before, but still remains constricted. And I don't think it has opened any further or easier in the last week. I return to the melody and catch a glimpse of Brett's puzzled face.

"I get it," he says. "I know that song."

I smile at his lie. I reach with my left hand, but it slips across the keys, mangling the G chord, slipping clumsily then into a C, the fingers unable to stretch as much as necessary, even for a simple note. I strike the keys hard with my right fingers, not caring now about the song, improvising, making my own music, allowing my left hand to bang out whatever it thinks sounds good. I close my eyes and rock my body, and my head sways up and down, strands of my hair dipping between the black and white keys. "Come on, come on," I whisper to myself. I forget entirely about Brett, about where I am. A part of me feels the discord of my music, the jangled notes, the random halting and starting, the arrhythmic pounding, but God, it is noise, clearer, stronger, louder than my voice, filling this vast room, filling Brett's ears and mine. A raucous blast of energy, a declaration of existence.

A slight touch on my shoulder and the spell is broken. My fingers pause, I open my eyes, and Brett smiles over me. Behind him is a green-clad orderly.

"Thank you, Robert," Brett says. "Thank you, but this gentleman asks that you play quieter."

There is regret in his voice and in his eyes, a reluctance to stop me, I can tell.

"Thank you," he says again, and I believe he means it.

I see Jodi often. She visits, sometimes steals me away for coffee. She badgers staff about my progress.

"There's usually not much success for a person who's been injured so long," says Clare, the head of the program. She speaks to Jodi across a long table, as though I'm not there, as though I can't understand. And I admit sometimes I feel like a guy in a foreign country, knowing just bits of the language.

"Over the years, bad habits develop in the way they do things, how they compensate for their losses," Clare says. "So we need to break old habits and develop new ones. It's not easy when you're working with people who need lots of repetition to learn even the most basic skills."

So progress is minimal. That's the gist of it. And the rate of progress is not likely to improve. The time will come when they will no longer be able to justify spending the state's money on my rehabilitation.

"But you're still evaluating him," Jodi says. "Robert has more potential than many of my other clients. For instance, his memory's not nearly as bad as the others. He even remembers small details, things I forget. Like he always remembers names, and if I promise him something, he reminds me of it the next time I see him."

"He obsesses on specifics," Clare says.

And so on, they debate my immediate future. Amazing to me how little say I get, though I'm always eventually asked my opinion, for ideas of what I'd like to do. My ideas are usually ignored or paid lip service to. I end up getting to choose between options committees have figured out before they've spoken with me.

Yet there are things here about Transitions I don't want to lose, the attention maybe, and I feel like I belong, as though these people care, and though I get tired of their constant badgering and harassing and directing, at least I am never bored here, not stuck in the dreary monotony of the day program, not forced to sit alone or to try to communicate with guys who have a harder time putting together words than I do. Here there is staff everywhere and always attentive.

And the other patients are on a higher level than back home. I suppose their minds are scattered some; they wander around some, but most can walk with help and talk plainly, and they're talking about getting jobs and returning to their real lives. I sense a guarded hopefulness here.

Jodi sits with me on a couch, at first just watching me, her chest occasionally heaving with long sighs, her stare unnerving me, and I hang my head like a bashful puppy dog. She has defended me. I imagine her in armor, a Joan of Arc, climbing the battlements, risking hot oil and arrows, clambering over the wall, reaching for me as I fall backwards from the parapets. Our hands grasp, our fingers lock. Is she strong enough to hold me, to pull me up safely? I stare back at her eyes.

She feels unnerved now. She blushes and fingers the top button of her blouse, then pulls her skirt down across her knees.

"You said nice things about me," I say.

"I said all true things about you. Listen, Robert. This Transitions program isn't going to be easy. You have to work hard to show them what you're capable of. Like I said, no miracles are going to happen, but I think you've got a lot of room to grow, a lot of things you can improve on."

"Okay, Jodi," I say. I continue to stare into her eyes, the blue of the sky above Flathead Lake in the summer. Her words, like the glistening strands of her hair, shower between us. I am lost in the cadence of her whispered declarations.

"Well, you're a wonderful man, Robert. Smart and funny and sensitive."

"Jodi," I say. I float on her words, her praises. I think of the Mission Mountains topped in sparkling white, emerging from the plains on a blue spring day. I think of tulips opening for the dawn sun. My heroine. "Jodi," I say, and reach for her hand, lean forward.

"I want you," I stutter.

"What?" she asks and leans away.

I sit up straight and swallow. I speak my words slowly, "I love you, Jodi."

My right hand floats low through the air, sneaking under her gaze and grabs her knee. My grip is strong from years of wheeling my chair, from dead-weight transfers. "I can stick my finger up you."

"Robert, no," she says firmly and stands up, breaking from my grip. Instantly I realize my mistake, and I'm reduced to being a bashful dog. I glance up to see the disappointment in her face, and I want to cry.

"I'm sorry, I'm sorry, sorry, sorry," I lament, knowing it may be too late. I remember what has happened in the past after such incidents. Women I thought were my friends distanced themselves, were repulsed at my touch and my thoughts. Now Jodi has just such a look in her eyes, and the corners of her mouth draw down in sad disgust. My judgment, they say, is impaired. And again I prove it. How can I deceive myself so much as to imagine my acceptability to a normal woman?

"Forget it," Jodi says, with considerably less warmth than she had been displaying. She frowns and makes an excuse to leave.

"Please don't tell," I say before she goes. "I want to stay in Transitions."

"I have to tell, Robert," she says. "How can they help you if they don't know what your problems are?"

"But they'll kick me out."

"I won't let them kick you out. But I've got to tell. For your own good."

Funny how everyone seems to know what's my own good.

The next day I'm scheduled for a double session with the psychologist, and later Brett tells me I'll be attending a weekly group for head-injured men where they discuss, among other things, sex and relationships.

Ellen has trouble with this section. She meets with me twice a week, sometimes at Transitions, sometimes at the group home.

"I feel inadequate," she says. "I'm not doing you justice anymore. It's so cold and opportunistic, trying to make art out of your life. And it's so bizarre to edit what you write about me, to edit my own words as you've remembered them."

"I have the tape recorder," I remind her.

"Still, it's not real. We're still editing. Maybe you should just stick to poetry; forget the book. Poetry is more suggestive and allows more room for the readers to imagine. It evokes emotions and leaves it at that, without going into personal details. With this prose, I'm afraid I'm editing your reality and making it more understandable, more palatable than it really is. I'm using you, and worse, I feel I'm lying about it."

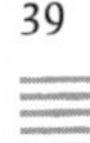

"I don't understand," I say.

"I'm not getting it right," she cries. "Look at this stuff about Jodi. I feel I'm invading your space, yet on paper, it comes out too clean. It all makes too much sense."

Ellen goes on about truth and manipulation and her vague guilt about latching onto my story.

"Shut up," I say. I need to write and I want her to help translate what I've got to say, to communicate it so I can be understood.

"By the way, since you started Transitions," she says and tries to smile, "your speech is much clearer."

"Write this," I say, and we try a new arrangement. She sits at the keyboard as I dictate.

Ellen sighs and types. She looks older than what I remember, the wrinkles in the corners of her eyes more pronounced. I wonder if she gets enough sleep, though I don't ask. I don't know what she does away from me. She stops her typing in the pause my mental wanderings have created, and as if reading my mind, she says, "My granddaughter has come to visit. She's about the age of your son."

This makes me uncomfortable, emphasizing as it does that according to our ages, I could be her son. I don't want this.

"She lives in Seattle with my son and his wife," she says. "They'd like to live here again, but there's so many more opportunities for work in Seattle."

I want to ask if she misses them, but it seems a stupid question, and I don't really want an answer. I want to get on with my writing about my life.

"Distances are hard," she says, "with family. I've tried e-mail. That helps me to forget the loneliness."

And so does volunteering, I think. She looks at me with large eyes, reaches and squeezes my good hand, then mumbles something, perhaps an apology of some kind that she is revealing this private information.

"Let's go now," she says. "What do you want to write next?"

8

"Where do you go?" Lorna's eyes question me. I have been avoiding her in the evenings and on weekends, as well as one wheelchair person can avoid another in the same house.

"Do you want to play Crazy Eights?" she asks one evening before dinner, and I beg off, claiming exhaustion, which is neither completely true nor completely false. Transitions' days have kept me so busy, that often I'm exhausted when I get home.

"Or, Robert, we could watch *Wheel* in my room? Definitely?"

"I can't, Lorna, not tonight."

"Where do you go in the day?" she asks, though I know I've told her a hundred times already.

"Transitions," I say, knowing this answer won't satisfy her any more than before.

She says a few words, but they're so garbled I can't understand.

"What? Can't you speak clearly, Lorna? Swallow before you talk."

"Can I go with you in the day?" she asks.

"It's not for you," I say. "It's for head-injured people."

I can see she doesn't understand my words, so I just turn away.

"I miss you," she says to my back, speaking as plain as any normal person might. I won't look back, but I imagine her begging eyes, a quivering lip perhaps, eyelids drooping and shutting the light out.

I retreat to my room, close the door, slip back, as I do, into my own thoughts, trying to piece together memories of Transitions, trying to lock into my mind images of Brett and Clare and the others. A draft seeps through the cracked window of my room, rustles my hair, and a smile creases my face. I remember a student's film when I was in college, a short film of cookies making themselves. Flour rises from the canister like a white powdery water spout, spiraling into a large bowl. Then sugar flows from a shaker like a waterfall, and pats of butter leap from a plate into the bowl. A spoon, unaided by any hand, mixes the batter. And then two eggs float in the air, knock themselves on the side of the bowl, and spill their insides, and the spoon mixes vigorously. Chocolate chips march then in single file along the table, leaping one by one into the bowl, till an army of them dots the batter, and the spoon folds them in, in patient, steady beats, with an amount of care that seems gratuitous. I remember this well. Once the ingredients are ready, the batter breaks like cells dividing, spoonfuls leap and settle onto a greased pan, and I wonder about the mystery of these ingredients mixing together of their own free will, to become a much more complex and delicious whole than their individual parts. Then I am overcome with sorrow that this batter, so well put together, is to be separated into individual cookies, to be baked and eaten. Would these dollops of batter have marched so lightly to their fate, to be part of the mix, if they had known how their perfection would culminate?

Images of Jodi invade my mind. Is this love? I remember some of my occasions with women before I was injured, but can't recapture the feelings. All I recall of John's mother is a cascade of raven-colored hair. Even times when I have stared at John, hoping something of his features will spark a remembrance of her face, her walk, nothing comes back. Except that long hair, like a trail of crepe paper black, streaming across my brain.

I never seem to have trouble recovering Jodi's image, and since Transitions I have only become more obsessed, more ridiculous with the notion I might actually be able enough again one day to be recipient of her love. Then I remember how I last treated her. I'll beg her forgiveness. Next time I see her I'll grovel. She must not be angry; she must not leave me.

I look at my walls, mostly bare except for pictures of family, cheap posters, and a framed print of pintos. I must have liked horses very much at one time. By the bed is a shelf of books I used to read—textbooks, music books. I'm not sure how they got here, how they survived the time between the accident and now. I don't much remember the hospital days, and the nursing home I prefer not to think about. It is all darkened halls and black rooms, and moans and wrinkled people roaming the halls in wheelchairs and walkers with urine smells and the fear I fit in only too well. "I am lost, I am lost." I don't know if I ever said the words, but I remember the feeling as a mantra daily, hourly, and "Mama, Mama, where are you?" and "Where am I?" What happened to my world? I couldn't express myself then, not that I'm any great shakes at it now, but it was worse then, buried, I felt buried, and the horror of the nurse's aide coming, in white, but a dark white. Somehow my memories darken even the brightest colors—and the sponge baths, and oh, I remember darkly a young aide . . . what did I do? what did I do? I'd never see her again. Nothing too terrible, I should think. And what did she think, undressing me? rubbing me? exploring me? Anyway, I was often alone. That's the terror of it: the absence of communication. Despite all the scurrying and chimes and false smiles in the halls, I know the boundaries of walls and long corridors, like nightmares when I wheel the spaces and examine the cracks of the plaster, hoping for an out, for a button or a door, finding nothing but a long shadowy white tunnel, filled with groans and calls of the elderly, the crippled, the trapped.

These are times when I think I have come far, though there remain times when I think I have far yet to go. Transitions provides a door I must rush through before it closes. Though I feel so unstuck in time, I also sense time closing down on me. I've got to work; I can't be distracted. Oh, there are times when I fear I have come as far as I ever will.

My God will you help me now, if I say I believe in You?

Lorna makes sure to sit next to me at dinner, refuses all staff's attempts to help feed her, and she stares at me. Across from me is a mirror, set up in a chair, an idea from Transitions so I will be careful with how I'm shoveling in my food, taking it slow, chewing each bite at least fifteen times, remembering to swallow, doing all the little things they've taught me, especially paying attention to the mess I create on my face and clothes.

“Robert, can you help me?” Lorna asks.

I look around, give her a stare like, “Are you talking to me?” She has green bits of food on her chin and down her blouse. Jennifer hovers behind us. “Robert has to pay more attention to his own eating,” she says. “I can help you, Lorna.”

“Yeah, let them do it,” I mumble, and a pea tumbles from the corner of my mouth onto my lap. “Goddamn, Lorna,” I say and slam my fork on my plate.

“Okay, Robert,” Jennifer says and moves Lorna and her food down the table away from me. I look into the mirror, not sure what to do with the unsmiling, untidy face that stares back.

9

Male Call, they've labeled us. Every week for an hour we gather apart from those women so prevalent in our disabled lives—the women who accept the low pay and nasty chores of personal care. We are invaded by women, and yet while they know us in intimate detail, we are allowed to get only so close to them.

Doctor Larry, the psychologist, sits so smilingly at the conference table, so warmingly he speaks to us, his teeth like toilet bowl porcelain after a flush. He's so slick we want to be like him.

Clustered around him are Brett and five clients, including myself. Freddie's another head injury, not nearly as bad off as me. He walks fairly steady and talks clearly, and he tells the best meanest jokes of anyone.

"How do you know a blonde's been in your refrigerator?" he asks the group, then speaks without waiting for an answer: "Lipstick on the cucumber."

I admit I don't get it, but everyone laughs, and I can't help but laugh too, giggle like a girl, my face flushed, my head bobbing up and down, my hand over my mouth, and drool seeping between my fingers. We, professional and client alike, are bonding in male embarrassment, sharing a vengeful reprieve from the women who surround us, and it all feels vaguely guilty and dirty, like sneaks at a *Playboy* at night, under the covers with a flashlight, when as far as Mom and God know, we've long ago fallen asleep. I keep laughing after the others have stopped. The more I try to stifle, the worse it gets, as any schoolboy knows. And my problem is, after all, no control. "Sorry, sorry, sorry," I say, "I'm too silly." And Doctor Larry understands, even breaks into a smile himself again, even relaxes for a minute with me—I mean, a full sixty seconds!—before correcting himself, putting us all back on task.

Our task: to explore our sexual feelings, our frustrations. Ah, women.

"I had this woman once," Freddie launches off on another story of ancient conquest, till redirected by Doctor Larry. Freddie shifts stories almost in mid-sentence, "There's this girl near where I live with red hair and long legs," he says. "She wears these short shorts."

"What's her name?" Doctor Larry asks.

"I don't know. Call her Lisa. I haven't actually met her. She's got this body . . ."

"So you've never talked with her?"

"I guess not, but she's so hot, man. I love watching her, thinking about her and me."

"Hold on, Freddie. Get out of the fantasies. Let's stick with reality," Doctor Larry counsels.

"Reality sucks," Freddie says. "I'm this brain-injured guy with a limp, I can't run without falling on my face, I have trouble remembering what day it is, and everybody says I got no control of my temper. I can only talk to this babe in my mind."

"Fantasies are healthy," Doctor Larry says, "as long as they stay in our minds and we don't act them out," and here he looks over at me, "but sometimes it's important to confront our reality, test it out. This woman, Freddie, might be nice, might be accepting of you, but you've got to get to know her, beyond her body."

"She wouldn't want nothing to do with me."

"She could be a friend."

"I don't want a friend, Doc. I want a lay."

"First things first."

"Easy for you to say. You're gonna go home to your wife tonight, aren't you, Doc? Gonna bonk her good, aren't you?" Freddie's voice gets loud and deep. His words spit into the air, fill the open center among us.

“Hey Freddie,” I say, and try to rise out of my chair. I wave my fist at him. “Goddamn you, Freddie. You don’t talk to Doctor Larry like that.”

Freddie laughs at me and Doctor Larry sits, not moving, patiently waiting Freddie out, though Freddie yells, “You’re all assholes here, goddamn.”

Brett rises and walks to him, “You’re being inappropriate, Fred. If you don’t stop right now, you’ll have to leave the group.”

“Who wants this idiot group anyway? You’re all a bunch of pussies.”

“Let’s go, Freddie.” Brett grabs his arm and helps him up. Freddie stands, then shakes off Brett.

“Don’t touch me. Don’t fucking touch me. I’m leaving. I don’t want to stay with this bunch of losers.” He leaves, followed by Brett. We hear more shouts, more anger even after the door closes.

“Sorry, guys,” Doctor Larry says.

“It’s n-not your fault,” says Luke, another client. He’s in a wheelchair. He talks slow, with a stutter and a slur but you can understand him fine. “It’s that d-damned Freddie.”

“He’s just expressing his frustrations,” Doctor Larry says.

“Yeah, yeah,” I say. “So how do we say what we want without going off the deep end?” I’m feeling all mixed up, angry at Freddie but feeling sorry for him too.

“Be courteous,” Doctor Larry says. “People will be your friends.”

“But I-I can play nice f-forever,” Luke says, “The g-girls are polite and s-sit with me and answer m-me, but just for a couple m-minutes; like they’re doing a-a job. If I ask f-for anything more, l-like to go to lunch or for a w-walk, or whatever, th-they make up excuses, they r-run.”

“You have to be yourself,” Doctor Larry says. “Relax and let things happen.”

“N-no,” Luke says. “No n-normal woman wants a-anything to do with us. P-period. That’s Freddie’s point, D-Doc,” Luke says and shifts himself up in his chair, anxiously. “This is the r-reality. I’m a hundred times w-worse off than F-Freddie. What chance do I g-got?”

“I don’t know,” Doctor Larry says quietly, “except you’ve got to keep trying, to stay open, to overcome the barriers. That's what we all do, even those of us who aren't injured. Your situation isn't unique, just different. But you have to start by seeing women as more than objects of your lust."

There is, there is, there is, I think, a woman waiting patiently for me. I never feel more trapped than when I watch a woman, some new staff maybe, wisping quietly around me like cigarette smoke I can see but can't grab, who coos to me in softened words, who urges me to bathe, to eat, to sit, to smile, to play, yet always retreats when I try to connect, when I wheel too close. These evasive female caregivers of our lives. The women of our intimacies. We must keep professional distance, you know, even while they transfer us naked in and out of bathtubs and wash around our testicles. Thwack. They flick our erections with their fingers, causing us to shrink because it is inappropriate for us to become excited, to swell with lust. They can't censor my dreams, though I hate myself for crossing the barriers in fantasies because I know I mean nothing to them in reality.

What, what is her name? That girl from years ago, my son John's mother? I see her in glimpses, images of her I make up. I think there is some memory, some vaguely remembered feeling of intimacy. It was no one-night stand. It baffles me that I can pretty well retrieve whatever I want from my long-term memory, but cannot retrieve her, which makes me wonder if there is something beyond my injury operating here, causing me not just to forget, but actually to repress. It feels sometimes, especially when I am with John, when he moves a certain way or turns a certain phrase, that I am nearly able to recall her, when her image seems about to emerge from the mists of my thoughts. But she remains elusive and free. Where is she?

"No woman will come to me, and I can't talk clearly enough," I say to Doctor Larry. "I can't think clearly enough. I've got to show what I feel."

Doctor Larry asks me to slow down and to repeat what I've said.

"If I don't force myself on them," I say, "I don't ever have a chance of getting a woman."

"You have to be appropriate, Robert," Doctor Larry says. "We all have inappropriate feelings at times, but you can't attack a woman."

"I have no other chance of getting what I want," I say.

“You puzzle me, Robert. You have a successful sexual relationship with a special friend at the group home. You should be happy. What more do you want?”

I have Lorna, I know, and a voice inside tells me I should be grateful, I should be satisfied, thrilled even. But I suspect Lorna accepts me for the same reason I accept her. There is no other game in town; no one else will have us. Yes, there is something genuine between us, but I keep wanting more, better, which makes me feel like slime. I wonder if Lorna loves me or does she pity me, simply put up with me?

What more do I want? I laugh at Doctor Larry, since my mind doesn’t work quick enough to describe, to enumerate what I want, to summarize it all neatly in a package he might understand. What I want is acceptance from normal people, because that would translate into normalcy for me. I want as mine the beauty the rest of the world judges to be beautiful. I want to fit into the standards of the normal world, beyond pity and condescension or revulsion.

I want a world more. A home, a white picket fence, my son John, and my wife bending over me, her breasts sighing in my face as she stoops to kiss me, and I rise like a gladiator from a chariot, bear her in my arms, manfully climb the stairs to our second-story master bedroom, where our lovemaking . . .

No, I am not so foolish as all this. These are rubbish fantasies. I must focus for a few minutes here, keep my attention on the question: what more? Beyond Lorna, yes, but not necessarily beyond my wheelchair, not beyond my memory and speech problems, not beyond my injury. These are mine forever.

“Stay within reality,” Doctor Larry advises.

But dream, I think. Because as of yet, reality has not been stretched to its limits.

I love Lorna. I am grateful for her. I don’t know why I keep reaching beyond her. I don’t know even what I seek.

“Robert, you must be appropriate in how you express your feelings. You can choose to control how you act.”

Maybe, but I don’t want to do this now, and I’m much too good at evading to be trapped so easily.

“Sorry, Doc, but my memory is so bad. I don’t remember anything from the last few days.”

“Don’t treat women as objects,” he rumbles on, like a wave gathering in the midst of the ocean. Someday he might break on shore, but not today.

I wonder if Lorna will feel well enough tonight that she and I might talk a little, watch TV in her room. Maybe if she’s well I can scramble into her bed for an hour or two. But she’s been sick a lot lately.

10

I sit lonely in this corner, near the metal and vinyl kitchen chair that has been placed in Lorna's room, out of sync with the bed, the dresser, the other bedroom furniture. When no one else is here, the chair keeps watch. And Lorna is sick again today, another Saturday with her in bed, propped upright, asleep or awake, the TV flickering its pictures and sounds, whether watched or not. Does a TV broadcast news if there's no one there to see it?

I do my time in the room that's become queer-smelling with ointments and lotions, and I talk in nonstop chatter, except for occasional rallies by Lorna, when she says, "Definitely," or says my name or the name of one of her kids. I swear she smiles when I touch her cheek or slide a hand under the covers. They've begun the watch, staff say, and I say they're all crazy. She's just more tired than usual. A few days of rest will revive her, and Lord knows, she has plenty of days here for rest. Do not, do not count her out yet. I know her better than most. Treat her normal and she'll revive.

Lorna. Do you remember days of sun? Days in forests, near the river, on accessible blacktopped paths? Fish breaking the surface of the water, ripples billowing in circles outward towards the shore where our wheels are locked on the tar? Do you remember our talks then of homes and children and warm fires when it's cold and bitter outside?

I don't remember either. We've made it up as we've gone along. You and I, Lorna. How much will only remain in our imaginations, continually remade?

I am right, it turns out, even to my own surprise, as Sunday breaks and she rises, well enough to be in her chair, and I go with her for a walk down our street, a small side street, away from heavy traffic, in a quiet neighborhood, where the neighbors have stopped bothering about us long ago, and the stares are only occasional and usually from children who keep their distance, who cannot conceive, though their eyes tell them otherwise, there are people with legs who cannot walk, with mouths whose lips cannot pour the words out straight. Jennifer pushes Lorna, and I wheel with my good hand and foot.

"Maybe staff can take us for a drive," I say.

"Definitely," Lorna says but doesn't look at me.

"Maybe we can have a picnic," I say.

"I can't understand you," she says.

I repeat a half-dozen times till it seems to register. We stop at a corner and face each other. She looks as sad as anyone I've seen, and beautiful with the sadness, I think. Look at her brown eyes, growing larger in her face by the day. She will be well again, and I will rise from this chair, with rehab help, and our future will be under ponderosa pines, near babbling rivers, and her children and grandchildren will laugh at the stories we tell about the days we escaped from chairs, from group homes. Lorna is getting better. I can see it, and I yell this at the top of my lungs, so that Jennifer moves Lorna back from me, slightly alarmed, yet calmly aware of my habits. Lorna speaks, but so softly I can't hear, so softly I'm not even sure she's making any sound at all. Her eyes are begging, like a dog hoping for a scrap, and it's all I can do not to cry, to steer my thoughts back to the reality that matters. "Let's go," I say, as slowly and clearly as I can manage. "On a picnic by the river. Someone will take us."

"Look at me," her eyes seem to say. "See me."

"We've got to get back home," Jennifer says. "Lorna's worn out."

How is it these staff presume to know us better than we know ourselves?

They speak of death, these sleek able-bodied folks. In the evening as Lorna sleeps, Jennifer speaks with me in the kitchen with those hungry eyes of sympathy that seem never to rest.

"Robert, the doctor says Lorna could die within a month. She's deteriorating fast."

"I don't think so. She was doing fine today. We had quite a long trip outside, and tomorrow I'm taking her to the mall."

"She has good days," Jennifer says. "But they'll be less and less. There's hospice counselors who are willing to talk with you about Lorna, if you'd like."

"She's just been tired lately."

"No, Robert; she's dying."

Even though I see the pain in Jennifer's eyes, hear her cracked slow speech as she tells me this, she is somehow above it all. After Lorna dies, after we all die or are shipped off to other places, Jennifer will walk home on two good legs and with a sound head to family and pets. Has she ever fallen like I have? Wakened after a long long pause and wondered what she's missed, wondered where she's been? Such a long hard blank in my life, or maybe I should say in between two lives, one real, one disabled. In my worst moments what I fear most is that Death is nothing but a long hard blank, no tunnels of light, no dead family on the other side, no resurrection nor salvation. Times when I wonder why I pray and doubts creep in among my meditations. At times in the bath when I am completely alone and the house is quiet, I can escape the rustle of thoughts and feel my white sheet of a soul reaching up high, expanding across my mind, whitening everything, and I feel close to a connection to something beyond me. But a noise or a random thought seeps in and I fumble. The whiteness shrinks, havoc is let loose again in my brain. Again I become unstuck and confused.

Lorna should not fall into that long hard blank of death. Not yet anyway.

On Monday I pretend to be ill. I complain long and loud enough that staff relent and let me stay home. Lorna again feels good enough to be out of her room, even to be wheeled to the backyard where staff and residents have begun planting peas and cucumbers, carrots and onions.

The morning sun haloes her head, and she smiles. I say hello, but I don't think she hears; she is in another place right now. After a silence, she turns her head, looks surprised to see me there.

"Robert, I had a garden, definitely," she says. "I have two girls and a boy. Have I ever shown you their pictures? They're such beautiful kids. And my house, have you ever seen my house? Tucked away in the woods with a redwood deck and young cedar trees guarding the back. We had lots of deer, and I saw a mountain lion once. I kept the kids inside for a week after that, till I heard they shot a lion down the road a little ways. Do you remember, Robert?"

"Sure," I say.

Lorna raises a shaky empty hand to her mouth as though trying to feed herself. I grab a plastic bottle with a straw from a picnic table and hold it near her mouth. She sucks but then coughs and spits out the thickened formula. I put the bottle down and hold her hand.

"What do you think, Robert? Are we lucky to be here now? Such a beautiful day. I think I smell lilacs."

"Yes, Lorna," I say, and can't think of anything else though I feel there's a lot more that could be said.

"Nothing hurts this moment," she says. "If I sit just like this and think good thoughts."

"See, Lorna, you're getting better. Tomorrow we'll go out. We'll celebrate."

"I'm exhausted," Lorna says. "Definitely. It's been a long day."

"It's only morning," I begin to tell her, but she dips her chin, her eyes close, her breathing becomes regular and deep and, like that, she is asleep.

She is asleep for a long time. On Tuesday, nurses come and attach tubes. She will be fed by tube, medicated by tube. Her face is contorted. She doesn't speak more than a word at a time. I sit by her into the night and try to pray.

II

Brett takes me skiing, the last day of the season, when trees are budding in the valley, but snow still lingers on the mountains. Sun sneaks through tall pines, streaks the snow which has fallen overnight, which desperately tries to resist the melting rays. It persists white and fine, wet and sloshy, then dissolves into puddles at the mountain base, an altogether glorious day for someone like me, so rarely do I get outside the city.

Wait. Ellen says this skiing trip needs more introduction. I disagree, but it seems lately I've resisted a lot of her suggestions, and I feel now like indulging her. Sometimes at Transitions, we do things just for fun. That is rehab too, Brett says. I knew Brett was a skier, and he volunteers at Marshall Mountain, the local ski resort, where there's a program in which volunteers help disabled people ski. So I asked Brett for a day on the slopes, a trip outdoors, though I haven't skied since before my accident, oh so many years ago.

It's not exactly skiing, but comes the closest I will ever get. Imagine me, with assistance, lifted from my wheelchair into a chairlift, strapped in and held onto by Brett, rising above the snow-dotted treetops on Marshall Mountain into a cloudless blue sky in the orange heat of the sun itself. It's me above ground, feet dangling. For a moment I daydream of slipping the nylon belt, eluding Brett's arm around my shoulder, falling, my arms and legs weightlessly perfectly spread, my body drifting gently like an opened parachute, following the mountain slope that continues down forever, so I never land. I live painlessly mobile hovering in space just above the cold ground. Imagine it.

The chairlift pauses long enough at the summit to deposit me and Brett, who works fast and efficiently to release me into the waiting arms of his accomplice. They have done this often before, expertly transferring folks from chairlift to adapted sled, so easily and quickly my feet fairly whisper over the snow, a faint white dusting lifted by our flurry of action.

"Brett," I rasp, out of breath from the experience. He leans over me to strap my body into the sled that has skis for runners and a cushioned raised seat. His breath puffs in little steam clouds before my face.

"Brett," I say again, peeking over his shoulder at the steep way down. He smiles at me, his face close to mine, our breaths now mingled between us. My eyes must betray my fright, because suddenly Brett's face breaks into concern. His words are meant to soothe, but it's been a long time since I've traded my chair for anything more daunting than a living room recliner. And I haven't stared down such a slope since . . . since when? I experience a vague feeling of vertigo. Images of blue empty space swirl like snow crystals inside my brain. I have stared down mountains before. Falling. Weightless. My prayers are always a descent.

There must be something funny about my frightened face because Brett laughs even while trying to reassure me. He reminds me I asked to try this, that, believe it or not, I'm on this mountain voluntarily, though now the only thing I can think of is how to keep what's left of my body intact. Surely Brett won't allow me down this mountain. There's been a mistake. A joke, played on the dumb head-injured guy. Okay, it's funny, guys. Let's go home now.

Brett can't understand a word I say, and I'm not listening to him anymore. At least he stops laughing, and his face is back to looking concerned. I can see he wants me to make this trip. Even as we speak through each other, a guy on skis named Cullen settles in front of me, attaching lines to himself that stretch back to my sled.

I sit up straight, swallow, breathe in, then bark, "No," as loud and clear as I can, but Brett shakes his head while he tethers himself with a strong cord to the back of my sled. He'll follow Cullen and me, acting as our emergency brake. "It's happening, Robert," he says.

"We've done this hundreds of times with others. It's safe." But he signals Cullen to wait.

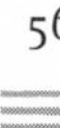

"Robert," he says, and begins a string of persuasions I don't recall word for word, but the gist is I need to take the risk, I need to soar beyond the wheelchair, beyond my definitions and others' definitions of myself. Maybe the physical challenge will stimulate my motivation to take on other challenges. Etc. Then he says, with earnestness, "Robert, it's a damned lot of fun. The most thrilling ride you'll ever take. Do it."

And I do, it seems. I don't remember quite agreeing, but I definitely lose my will to resist. Before me, the blue-jacketed Cullen lifts his poles and powerfully pushes off, me in tow, Brett behind, a fine spray of snow swirling before my eyes. Cullen sways and turns, scissors across the slope, down the mountain, and though I see skiers on each side pass us, it feels like we are going faster than I've ever gone anywhere before. I feel the whoosh of wind against my face, my body hit with a rush of adrenaline, my stocking hat spilling off my head, my hair suddenly escaped and streaming behind me. I hear a howling sound, and it takes a moment to realize it's me. It's me skiing down a slope. I feel the sled tilt, lift slightly on one runner as we careen and turn, and nearly spill, Cullen looking behind several times, smiling beneath his eerie reflective goggles. Brett tries to slow us several times from behind, but it's as though I'm tethered to a madman in front, slicing at high speed down a slope, and loving it. I pound on the bar of the sled that helps hold me in. I scream, "faster, faster." I revel in the wind, the white dusty world filtering past, peripheral glimpses of pines marking my swift progress. This is the closest I will get again to falling, to being free of my body, lunging into that weightless space I dream about. I let go of the safety bar in front of me and stretch out my good right arm high above my head; I hold my gnarled spastic left hand into the wind, and I swear I feel the wind pry it open, so that air whistles between my fingers.

I laugh and yell, and ignore Brett's warnings to sit back, to hold on. He tries to slow us down, and I try to rise in protest, feeling maybe I have suddenly been given back my ability to move my body at will. But my efforts topple the sled, and I go rolling head first into the snow, my face ground in as the sled rolls on top of me, and I see

Cullen tripped up himself, his long skis spilling over his head and heels, his body crashing hard. Brett whiplashes around us, still tethered to the sled, till he tumbles and drags me and the sled with him. I roll over more than a few times, dragging Brett and Cullen, till finally I slide into a tree, stopped dead still nearly at the mountain base. Brett bounces up quickly and begins disentangling Cullen, who, once freed, helps Brett upright me and the sled. Brett spits out words, jumbling a scolding of me for not being careful with apologies for the spill. He pauses when he looks at my face, and I look down to see patterns of red blood melting into the snow.

"Geez, I'm sorry, Robert," Brett says. Cullen is quieter, madder, I suspect. "I don't think anything's broken," Brett says, inspecting my injuries.

"No," I say, and then I start laughing at Brett's worried face, at Cullen's angry stares, at the wind, the snow that is now eddying in a surprise whirlpool breeze.

"I want to do it again," I say. The trees bend in the wind. "Again," I say. I want to repeat and repeat the experience, to lock it in my brain cells. The rush, the freedom, the risk.

Cullen shakes his head, angry yet, but with a bemused look at me that reveals his suspicions of my sanity.

"Again," I say to Brett, who kneels on one leg next to me, scrutinizes my face, scratches his head behind his ear.

The trees bend, and Brett nods his head. "Okay," he says, "okay."

12

I dream of houses often, of houses and places I swear look familiar, but when I awake I can't identify them. Always there's extra rooms and long hallways, always doors opening, renewable adventures.

Last night I dreamt of walking with my dog, one I had on the High Line when I was a kid, a yellow Lab retriever, in a city I've been to though I can't name it, a big foreign city where there's old stone buildings and narrow streets. On top of a hill is an attraction the tourists for some reason ignore; you have to be an insider to know of it: Greek pillars and statues and tombstones and mausoleums—though this is not Greece. I walk up a steep hill to a complex of old brick buildings, churches and chanceries and hospitals all built tilted on the side of the hill. I scramble over and around a crumbling brick tower, almost falling a couple times, but am saved when I grab onto my dog's collar. When I am past the tower, a few local people are funneling into a museum entrance, but I don't have the money to pay, and I don't know what to do with my dog, so I can't get in. I can't get to the statues and stonework I know are at the top of the hill. But mostly I'm frustrated because I can't figure out what city I'm in.

I don't have a clue about my dreams, though I've tried to pin meanings onto them. Only rarely am I wheelchair-bound in them, though there often seems to be a chair near me.

I try over the weekend to meditate on my problems, while sitting in the corner of Lorna's room, she of the tubes and fatigue, of one-word sentences, and only glimpses of awareness. Definitely. She's of my real life here. I confuse what is dream and fantasy as I meditate and lose sight of what really exists. I can't empty my mind completely. I can't escape images of tunnels and torchlights flickering, of rocky mountain faces that loom, challenging, before me. I can't escape Lorna's occasional shuffling, a spasm now and then, a groan or a snicker, and who can tell if she's dreaming or awake, what level of consciousness she is in? Who can ever tell about any of us?

I'm interrupted. Three sullen-faced children with their grandparents come weeping in, remnants of her real life, before me. The adults briefly and tolerantly smile at me. The kids ignore me, but are trapped between me and their mother, nowhere to shift their eyes till Jennifer sneaks in and wheels me out. But I insist on sitting in the doorway, and I watch the exercises, the motherly fingers parting Lorna's thinning hair, the father's nervous cough just before he bends to kiss Lorna's forehead, the kids crying out loud, holding onto their mother's hands, both hungrily and angrily. It is so brutal and sweet a scene even I must turn away and leave them their peace. I retreat and let Jennifer close the door.

When they are gone, I am there again, in the corner, unsure why I keep so faithful a vigil this weekend. Lorna awakens once, long enough to speak: "Robert, you're definitely my man." I wheel nearer and grab her hand and smile at her, holding on before she disappears again. I want to be her family, her comfort, so I caress her cheek with my good hand, I smooth her blankets, I try to speak softly with pity in my voice. She alternates between smiles and grimaces.

I tell her what I remember of my skiing experience but see no flicker of interest in her eyes, just a furrowing of her forehead I attribute to pain or confusion or irritation with what I say. How dare I speak of a joyful activity as she deteriorates?

"Get up," I whisper through gritted teeth. "C'mon Lorna, let's get out of here." I pull a tube and grab her arm, and she gives a smile like I've never seen before, so otherworldly that it scares me back. Lorna, we can wheel towards the light, you and me. I advance again, unbuckle my seat belt, and shuffle a hand under her head. Please Lorna, remember our days and nights of not so long ago. I come to you by instinct more than memory, drawn to you, beyond any choice I make. I'm a man and I need you. Wake up!

I lean forward to kiss her, feeling excited and frustrated, leaning deeper into her face, and my chair scoots out from under me and my face falls heavily into hers, my knees hit the floor, and then I am sprawled on the floor next to her bed, cursing myself, trying to scramble up, reaching for my elusive, treasonous wheelchair.

Of course, staff is there immediately—if not sooner, as the saying goes—with horrified faces and wagging fingers of disgust and repudiation. Robert oh Robert oh Robert oh. A male staff lifts me and tosses me none too gently into my chair. Jennifer attends to Lorna with sighing whispers. Oh Jesus, I've screwed up again. Jesus.

Later Jennifer gives me the lowdown, that I can't be in Lorna's room unsupervised anymore. It's a liability thing, she explains, trying to soft-soap my idiot behavior, and what if her family knew, and she can't resist, just can't resist telling me more, preaching a little. It must have hit a moral chord for her, because here is what Jennifer says, reconstructed as best I can:

"Robert oh Robert, Lorna is dying. She's not competent anymore; she can't consent to any kind of sex. You've got to leave her alone." And Jennifer breathes hard, thinking she's done, but her face turns red and she blurts out: "Robert oh Robert, think of Lorna. I know you've got a good heart, but I can't believe you keep pushing yourself on Lorna considering the shape she's in. Think of others besides yourself." She literally bites her tongue and then shuts up, seeing I'm properly chastised, as I hang my head in wonderment that she can be so right and yet so wrong at the same time. But it's just a feeling and no way can I say in what she's right and in what she's wrong.

The next day is Sunday, and I'm in church again, singing oh singing till my lungs might burst and Jennifer whispering to me to keep it down, I'm embarrassing myself. But I can't stop, even after the organ stops. I think of Lorna dying in her room while I pray in church. Jennifer finally threatens to wheel me out if I don't shut up, and I am, finally, quiet. Why am I here praying for what? That Lorna not die, that her pain continue? I look around me at the pitying faces of the congregation looking at me.

Oh how I love Jesus, cleft for me. How great Thou art, how great I art.

13

Ellen visits me at my old day service in the computer room. I have been suspended indefinitely from Transitions.

I will describe what happened the day before, I tell Ellen. And despite her protests that I should be doing this myself, she types what I say into the computer

---

"What did you do over the weekend?" Brett asks, he and I in the activity room at Transitions.

"I don't remember." I'm in a sour mood.

"Look at your memory book," Brett says. "Didn't you write in it?"

"No." I lie about the memory book, a tablet in which I'm supposed to write down, or have others write down for me, events I'd like to remember. I don't remember details of the weekend, but I know Lorna's in that book, and I don't want to talk about her now.

"You've got to use your book," Brett whines. "You've got to try harder, Robert."

I struggle to reach behind to the pouch hung on my chair. With difficulty, and without a whit of help from Brett, I manage to extract the mangled tablet.

"Why are you pulling it out," Brett asks, "if you didn't write anything?"

I throw the book at him, catch him off-guard; it glances off his cheek.

"Okay," he says, rises from his chair, and walks around me. "I can't accept inappropriate behavior. There's got to be consequences."

"I'm no damned child," I spit out, but he doesn't understand.

"Maybe you need time by yourself," he says. "If you can't be appropriate, you can't be around people."

"To hell with you." He seems to catch what I'm saying now. Or near enough.

He leaves, shuts the door, and I sit there alone. Goddamn him and his whole program. What the hell do these people know, able-bodied as they are? What do they endure that comes anywhere close to what I endure? How can they know anything about what I live?

So who gives a damn if I don't use my memory book, or forget the bologna on a bologna sandwich, or if I ram an electric wheelchair into a wall, or if I compliment a girl on her breasts? Goddamn them all to hell and beyond.

What about my left hand, which is now stalled in its progress, that just won't stretch out any farther so when I sit at the piano, I still can't reach between octaves? But no one seems to care about that.

And maybe I don't care. Isn't this just a giant con game, a way to keep these professionals occupied and paid? They can't give me my memory back. They can't get me to walk again, or even cross a street safely. And what are the professionals doing for Lorna? What is it all for?

Near a shelf on the wall are small silver dumbbells, and on the floor are large brightly colored therapy balls. I kick a ball across the room, then pull down all the weights I can reach. I throw one dumbbell so it breaks a hole in the wall, and the crash brings staff running. I throw another weight at Brett, but it misses him and nicks the shin of a woman staff.

"Jesus, Robert," Brett breathes, as he holds my arms down. "What the hell's gotten into you?"

"Goddamn it. Goddamn, Goddamn." I yell but no one understands.

Later in the day, Jodi comes in, all made up and walking that bouncy walk she walks, smiling like all is sweet and roses, her eyes wide and unburdened by anything more than visions of what to buy her kids for their birthdays.

"Robert," she says in her whispery, syrupy voice, "you've got to leave here for a while. They'll decide later when you can come back."

"Damn them all," I say.

"You can't stay in Transitions unless you're making progress," she says.

"I don't care. Just get me out of here and out of the group home," I say.

"Moving into your own place depends on you showing good judgment and social skills. You can't throw stuff at people or make inappropriate remarks." When I give her a look of innocent protest, as if I don't remember what I've done, she says, "You know what I mean. Sometimes that memory of yours is very selective."

"Go to hell," I say.

"This is not how to resolve a problem."

"I don't want to be here anymore."

"We won't keep you here against your will. But if you fail here, it's back to the group home, for good." She pauses, straightens a crease in her skirt, then looks me in the eye. "So why did you blow up in here?"

"I don't know."

"I hope you haven't screwed up this chance."

"I want my hand back. I want to walk again. And think normal again."

"I told you when you came in here there would be no miracles."

"What about my hand?"

"Keep exercising it as much as possible. Push it down onto hard surfaces. Keep opening up the fingers."

"What's the doctor say?"

She sighs heavily. "He says it's probably opened up as much as it ever will. But you can keep trying."

"What about walking?"

"You need to stand more at the standing table. Get your legs strengthened and more limber. But I hear you've been refusing to stay standing for very long."

"It's boring, and it's not walking."

"Robert, you've got to cooperate."

"Shit."

"For now, I'm taking you back to the day service. It'll be a couple days before you can come back. If they take you back."

I look at her face, and my thoughts fade into fantasies—or are they some haunting memories?—of a soft kiss on my cheek from a woman as she leaves my bed. I can still feel the sweetness of the moment, knowing it is just that, a moment, and now that woman, whoever she is, is back in her own home, perhaps with a husband in a recliner, a son out fishing or inside playing Nintendo. All I have is that moment. A kiss as a memento of olden times.

"M-My wife," I stammer.

"You aren't married, Robert."

"What about Lorna?" I say.

"Is that what's bothering you?"

"No, there's nothing wrong." And I begin to laugh, and my laugh rolls like a locomotive chugging, building as it climbs a steep hill. I laugh loudly and inappropriately, showering the air in front of me with spit. I am not a good boy, and it is too damned funny. I can't say what, but it is just too damned funny, what these people know and don't know.

Ellen types for me my shower of words. "Get it down before I forget," I urge her. "There's something important here." But I get lost in thought, then focus on her reddened, veiny hands, her thick knuckles and fingers paused over the keyboard, and I tell Ellen to relax, I will type this in later. Her hands settle to her lap, one inside the other like a hot dog in a roll. Ellen has had her stories which she keeps mostly to herself, but occasionally she tells me a little. There was a husband or two and children now grown and living in other cities, and she's told me about a file drawer full of rejection slips from some of the best and worst magazines around the country. This writing life sucks at times, she says. So why, I ask her, do we scramble after the words, the images which, even if we get them right, are all but ignored by the world we try to communicate with?

"Because," she says, "sometimes we get them right."

A world screams inside me, a random reflection of the world that blurs outside of me. And tall ancient buildings collapse like Hollywood facades, crumbling inside me, and there I am, crippled fool, trying to rebuild constantly, as though I can beat time or the wrecking ball. My prayers are stones piled one by one atop each other, but they tumble often, so I repeat, pushing and struggling with the same stones day after day, my building never quite repaired. Still . . .

"Say something, Ellen," I tell her. And she begins by asking me how I feel, what can she do to help me get back to Transitions, till I tell her to shut up.

"Tell me about you," I say. "No one tells me about themselves. Everyone's too busy trying to document and fix my life."

She smiles and speaks about three or four children, and here and there, years of schooling, an escape from a marriage, writings and rejections and here she is, struggling with me, not altogether sure why, and can I be honest with you, she asks, and for some reason, I am proud of the moment. I realize how rarely people are honest with me when I am Robert, not the patient or client or object of condescension. "I don't know why," she says, "I keep coming back, why I pursue this project with you. I'm really afraid I'm screwing up something that feels important. And I can't tell you why this is important. Why do I want so badly to get into your head?"

"I don't know," I say. Living a life among paid caregivers, I have come to assume my right to be heard.

"I used to think it's because you're brain-injured," she continues, "that you have a unique voice, a unique take on the world because of your injury, but now that seems to be secondary. It's just you, the inside you I want on paper, and I don't think it matters at all if you're disabled or not."

Well, what does one say to all this? Especially if you're someone like me who can never wrap words around thoughts fast enough to keep a conversation going. She continues anyway, not waiting for my responses, communicating with me, not waiting like adults do for young children, you know how they wait, then coax out the answers they want.

It's all fine and dandy what she says. Believe me, Ellen, I am honored, but then my mind wanders, till I slam my left hand onto the countertop, forcing the fingers to spread. I thank you, Ellen, then wheel past you out of the computer room to the piano in the far corner, mostly unused except by me. I lean far over the keyboard, my cheek nearly resting on the black keys, and I play. Nothing really. No song, but my own improvisation. It is wild and jazzy and woefully incomplete, finally descending into banging low notes as the clumsy fingers of my left hand pound mercilessly, arrhythmically, jubilantly on the keys.

14

I am drenched with dreams of rain inside, thunder and electric jags that flash for too brief a second, promises that fade.

Back in Transitions after a week away, everyone treats me like a long-lost son, all forgiveness, like I've never left. After a week of boredom at the day service, I'm happy to be back, ready to try hard, to be good. I will do everything, everything they ask, and I won't flip out or lose my temper or say anything inappropriate. If I remember, that is.

Truth is, and I hate to admit it—don't realize it myself till I'm back here—being away is painful. I like these people, their relentlessly upbeat attitudes, their attention, the conversation, even the other patients, who at least aren't the same old, same old group home residents I've lived with, oh like forever. So give me room, clear space around that table there, guys. I'm back.

Brett's his old self, smiling at my return. With one hand, he massages my shoulder, asks how I am, says he had a long talk with Doctor Larry about me, and figured the program's failing me and not the other way around. Though the time out was good, he thinks, for me to value more what I'm doing here. Maybe.

So let's begin again, and we'll start right away, he says, with one of my goals.

He wheels me to Tonya, the physical therapist, who announces, "Okay, Robert, today we start walking."

Forgive me for not getting excited, for not jumping up and down, so to speak, I mumble, but these legs haven't been anywhere near working order for years, though I admit I've stood up, leaning on counters and such occasionally. You see, I can stand, like an emerging toddler, shaky with balance, never sure where exactly my legs are or what they might do, holding onto persons or furniture, but damned if I can go anywhere without promptly spilling in a lump on the floor, unable to get myself up again.

Tonya produces an aluminum walker and smiles at my frown. Images of the past flash inside me, toppling over and around these contraptions.

"I can't say how independent you'll ever be with this," she says, "but I'd like you to give it a try. It might be you'll only be able to use a walker with staff holding onto you, or guiding you, or just there ready to catch you if you fall."

"What's the point?" I want to say, suddenly feeling cranky again. I only mumble in ways I know they can't understand.

"This was one of your goals," says Brett. "I thought you'd be excited. What is it, Robert? Are you scared?"

Yeah, scared and you'd be, too. Sometimes, I think staff don't understand how hard a floor can be, carpeted or not, how there's times I don't want to get out of bed just because I don't want to face the effort needed to rise and transfer, the fear of falling heavily, of hurting yet another hand or limb or back or chest. Yeah, scared because though I want to walk, to be upright, to trash this wheelchair forever, they're not offering any guarantees here, and too much already my hopes outpace my abilities.

Brett locks the brakes on my chair, undoes my seat belt, both things I can do, and am usually encouraged to do myself, making me think Brett's more excited about this than I am. But damn, then I feel a lump swelling from my gut to my throat, an anticipation something wondrous is going to happen, that I am going to make a genuinely large stride towards health and happiness. It's not fair.

Leaning over me, Tonya places a wide colorful fabric belt around my waist—a gait belt—by which, when I am lifted, an aide can hold onto me. Behind me, her arm sturdy around me, Tonya lifts on the belt, and I feel my butt rise from the chair, my weight shifting to my legs, Brett to the other side of me, waiting with his arms slightly out, and it's a good thing he's there, because I slip, fall heavily back into

Tonya's arm, nearly trapping her hand under my butt. Brett helps lift from his side, allowing just enough room for Tonya to slip her hand and arm from behind me. She sets herself again, asks me to lean forward, and we try again, this time quicker and smoother till there I am, standing, not exactly straight, but bent and draped over the walker Brett holds steady under me. My legs wobble and my arms shake, but with help I stay on my feet.

"Come on, Robert, straighten up," Tonya says and tugs on my gait belt. And then I am straight for a second, maybe two. Then I can't feel my legs at all, or to be more exact, I'm not sure what they're doing, spasming, or knees locking, but what I do know, what I remember is tumbling back and sideways, landing heavily into Brett's arms, falling into the soft cushion of his lap as he stumbles under my weight, and there we are, him on the floor, me on top of him, and I want to swear up a storm, I want to tell these people to leave me alone, I've come as far as I'm going to, but damn Brett, he's laughing, like a dumb hyena, he can't stop. He's got one arm around me as Tonya tries to lift me to my chair, but then she catches Brett's eye and she's gone too, into her own giggles, and I want so much to be like them I can't do anything but laugh too, shake like a bowl of Jell-O sitting in Brett's lap, and God, but don't tears come streaming down my cheeks, and I think I've even wet my pants, and still we're all laughing, till other staff arrive, like the cavalry, to lift me. Brett's still chuckling as he accompanies me to the bathroom to change.

"I haven't wet my pants since . . . I can't remember," I tell Brett and this sets him off laughing again. We are all so silly, and I feel genuinely happy here at this moment, and anxious to get cleaned up, to try again to rise, to walk.

When a disabled man rises, where does he go? When he rises, there is nowhere to go but down, eventually. But oh the ride while it lasts. Tonya and Brett try again with me, and this time, I remain steady enough at the walker that I stand straight for at least a minute, before falling back almost smoothly into my wheelchair.

Jodi appears, to check on my progress, she says, and she smiles and touches my knee.

"We've got him standing," Tonya says.

"And how do you like being back in Transitions?" Jodi asks.

“Fine,” I mumble and try to stare into her eyes, but I drop my gaze. Something makes me ashamed. I don’t know what it is, but I don’t want to look at her. Coming unsummoned, then, surprisingly, are images of Lorna in her hospital bed at the group home.

“Come on, Robert,” Tonya says. “Let’s try again. Show Jodi what you can do.”

I sit, transfixed, my eyes down, focused on my left leg where a sudden spasm has antagonized my foot. “Damn,” I gasp through gritted teeth, and my thoughts turn back to Lorna. I rarely think of her when I’m at Transitions, and now I can’t lose sight of her, and these are no fanciful images of times I’ve never known with her. These are real images of her frowning in her pain, in her confusion, and mixed in are images of her and me seated next to each other, holding hands, laughing, talking, leaning across the arms of our chairs for quick kisses, like school kids sneaking small passions.

“Give me your foot.” I hear Brett’s voice, as from a distance though he’s right next to me; in fact, he’s leaning over and in front of me, with my foot in his hands, trying to untie my shoe. His breath flows to me on his words, smelling sour like pickles or onions.

“It’s okay,” I manage to say, but Brett has my shoe off now, and he massages the arch of my foot with hard swift rubs till the foot finally relaxes, becomes pliable, behaves, and settles into its more normal condition, which is with a slight inward turn at the ankle.

“He might need a brace,” Tonya says.

“I’ll call Orthotics,” Jodi says.

“Not an insurmountable problem,” Tonya says. “Robert, I need you to stand again. I want to see how your foot does with weight on it.”

And there I am again, upright, leaning on the walker, standing between Brett and Jodi. I feel her fingers on my elbow, a hand on my back. Tonya paces around us, examining me from different angles.

“In all the years I’ve known you, I’ve never seen you standing up,” Jodi says.

I’m shocked to find myself looking down into her eyes. I’m at least six inches taller than she is. I feel the playing field between us has been slightly leveled.

“Can you take a step, Robert?” Tonya asks, but I’m still pondering my sudden height advantage over Jodi. My knees start to shake; my left foot suddenly feels weak with the weight on it. “Watch out,” I shout a warning and tumble backwards, into Brett’s and Jodi’s arms. They stumble a little but are able to ease me gently back into my chair.

“Okay, Robert,” Tonya says. “I’ve seen enough for today.” She tells me and Jodi her plans to get a brace to support my foot and ankle and outlines a plan that would have me standing more and more each day at a standing table to strengthen my legs. “Walking is still a gamble,” she says. “From my work with you, Robert, I’d say you have the ability in your legs and your balance should improve with practice. But you’ll definitely need a brace and a walker. And even then, you might not ever be able to walk without staff helping you.”

“Do you want to continue with this?” Jodi asks. “It’ll be hard work to get just that far.”

I remember standing next to her. I remember looking directly into Brett’s eyes.

“Yes,” I say. “I want to walk.”

There’s a mystery here I contemplate at night alone in my room, listening to my tape recordings of the day and reading my memory book. I have stood before, since my accident, for even longer periods of time and steadier too. I’m told I once used to walk a few steps by holding onto kitchen counters at the group home, though I don’t remember. But standing straight today between Brett and Jodi has filled me with a serenity I haven’t felt in a long time, as though a hope has been actually realized. But it’s not the standing or the prospect of walking that excites me, but something more vague, too elusive for me to define. Standing upright next to Jodi is part of it, but so are the random images that flooded me about Lorna. Now what did they mean? When I got home I looked in on Lorna, even sat for a while with her, but she remained sleepy and groaning, and I’m not sure she knew I was there.

Here I am in my room with the curtains half-drawn and the last remnants of the day’s light casting deep shadows behind my bed and chair and desk.

Here I am, God, in wild spirits and energy, trying to capture the illusions you send, illusions that skirt around and skip through my fuddled-up brain. Today there was a perceptible rise in my state, not just standing but a different feeling, a beginning of an ascension. In a reversal of my usual habits, I started low and then rose, am still rising even as darkness falls, and now I close my eyes, and let the images flow, of me standing, of Lorna lying back, of Lorna smiling, resting finally after some pain somewhere quits its assault, and then I see a building rising from dusty rubble, putting itself together stone by stone, cemented with mortar, rising without the assistance of human hands. But cracks appear here and there, and suddenly from the dust come carpenters who surround the building, and work halts. They point and probe, then separate to confer in small groups.

Lorna. Her face overwhelms all other images. And then I'm in a dream; awake or not, I can't tell. But Lorna is up, in her wheelchair, I slightly behind, making slow progress, bent over a walker, Jodi and Brett behind me. I follow Lorna into a narrow cave that seems nothing but dark, but I hear deep within a thump, thump, thump, like a heart pounding, but too loud, too sporadically. We travel farther, and I think I see a sliver of light peeking through a cut in the rock, and accompanying the thumping then is a boy's voice. Is it mine? The boy shouting, playing, laughing, and the thump thump thump I recognize as a rubber baseball hitting the side of a house. Thump thump, it continues, even as I pause to listen, discerning now a peculiar rhythm to the thumps, a melody emerging. I turn to speak to Lorna, but see only wheel tracks on the floor of the cave, leading on, and Lorna nowhere in sight.

I wake up, and I feel keenly the desperate desire for a piano to play.

15

I feel like a stuck record, a needle locked in a groove, playing the same chords, the same words over and over. I can dream no fresh thoughts.

The flowers were late blooming this year though people say more splendid for the wait, or maybe just more appreciated. Does some resentment sink into the soul when spring comes late? If it can choose to be late this year, what's to prevent it from choosing not to come at all? I look at Transitions' calendar on the board where staff daily write the date. The large purple letters and numbers are messed up, dripping downwards like they are weeping, as June seeps away, tumbling into summer.

"Try a blank screen," Ellen says when I complain about my lack of things to write. "Darken the screen so you can't see what you write, then just type without thinking, without looking at what you're doing."

So I try it but I type so slow I can't possibly keep up with all the nonsense thoughts from my brain. Instead I find myself staring at the blank screen, zeroing my eyes into gray-black darkness, meditating, letting my brain take a holiday.

Why they come, their vigilance ongoing, I no longer know, but here it is near the Fourth of July and my parents, towing my son John along, are visiting again, sitting in the group home kitchen, talking of the High Line and home nonstop, and I am so impatient with it all I clutch my gut and groan. I have work to do. I stare through them and stay silent.

This visit is out of the ordinary. Mom writes and calls regularly, and I go home once or twice a year, but usually they come to me only every other year or so.

"Well, John wanted to visit, you know," Mom sputters in explanation.

I feel guilty that I don't want to see my son, and honestly it is not like me. They grill me with questions about my "progress." John looks at me with entirely too much expectation.

Finally I leave them at the table, wheel to my room, and shut the door. I transfer roughly from my chair to my bed, forgetting to set the brakes, barely making it as the chair scuttles backwards, away, out of my reach. I curl my legs to my chest and turn my back to the door.

I have no peace for long. Jennifer bursts in, stands hands on hips as I turn to face her.

"They've come a long way to see you," she says.

"Tell them I'm sick," I say.

"You tell them, Robert."

"I'm ashamed," I say. "I love them, but I don't want to see them now."

"Why not?"

"I don't know." I look in the mirror and see my drooling, slumped face, my weak, stricken body. "I've got work to do."

"They love you," Jennifer says, "as you are."

"No, they want me better. They want me different."

"At least visit with them for a while."

My dad walks in, in a gray-haired shuffle, baseball cap in hand, like a boy in a candy store asking for credit. Instinctively I sit up to face him.

"Son, maybe it wasn't a good time. Maybe we should have given you more notice."

"I'm sick," I say. As usual he doesn't understand me, just nods as though he does, and continues: "It ain't fair to John. He really pushed for this trip, and to be honest, it used to be we had to drag him kicking and screaming to come with us. If I was you I wouldn't turn him out just now. You never know with sons when they'll come back."

My mind goes unstuck, drifts back in time. I'm a small kid on two good legs, staring at a door between me and my parents, raised voices on the other side, then my father bursts through that door so quick my head is almost clipped as it swings out, and I reach a hand for him but get nothing but air. I call out, and he turns with a scowl and a creak of floorboards beneath his weight. He is the ugliest, most fearsome sight I have ever seen, and he turns again out a door leading outside, without a word or kind gesture. I stare at the door and wait.

He has not been a bad father. I remember that incident for its uniqueness. I watch him now, stooped with hands on knees, next to Jennifer, appearing tiny next to her. What accident, I wonder, has caused him to shrivel like my left hand? Ah, life.

I prayed at that door, kids' prayers from church: Hail Mary full of grace the Lord is with Our Father Who art in heaven hallowed be His name His kingdom come I believe in the Holy Spirit the Holy Catholic Church the world without end for these and all my past sins I am heartily sorry. Sorry.

In my long-term memory, Dad comes in and out of doors uneventfully for a lifetime. Except for occasions few and far between. Like now, when his entrance to my room portends more than the usual. Looking at him there beside Jennifer I consider him the saddest man in the world and realize too the frightening scowl on his face of so many years ago, the look I dread even in memory, was more of sadness than meanness. We are sad people, Dad, you and I.

He is there always, usually in the background, behind my mother, acquiescing to every dream she puts forth, nodding like the good husband, dutifully bending to the yoke, a small farmer and rancher before retirement. When I come home, he talks to me about the land and the high school basketball team and Old Man Chambers' goat and the bar on the corner, all like I was some normal kid come home from the big city, like I was my brother Cyrus, still able and sharp-witted. Except, my mother jokes, that he talks to me at greater length than anyone, though only at home, not here, just on his own comfortable turf. If what my mother says is true, I know why. He never waits for my answers, for my turn at conversation. He lacks the patience to understand me, so he has freedom to say what he wants. He can pour his heart out without fear of criticism, can believe I understand and sympathize with every word and emotion he expresses, like some best son, like the wife a man dreams of having. With me he can brazenly escape the High Line male taciturnity because though he speaks of male things—bars and land and sports and dirty jokes—I am not quite a man in his eyes. I am a passive audience, an absorber of monologue, of lost dreams, of next year's expectations. And I love it. I follow my dad like a dog at home, as much as I can, when he stays on smooth terrain my chair can navigate. I know the lowly position he keeps me in, the ignorance of my growth. I know too his love, his acceptance of me, his allowance of my presence.

He has been talking as I have been recollecting.

"And your mom, you know if you don't come back out, she'll fret and moan the whole trip back; then for months later, she'll complain to me about it."

"Shut up, Dad," I bellow. He doesn't make out the words and takes my reply as encouragement that he's on the right track.

"Your mom loves you. I know she can go on crazy about wishing things different, but it's just she always wanted things perfect. Even before your accident. She was never one to settle for ups and downs."

I give him a look and a deep groan so finally he takes notice and pauses.

"Dad," I say, clear enough.

"I think," he says haltingly, "maybe for their sakes, John's and your mother's, you might come out again." He pauses again and studies me. "For my sake too," he says. "I love you too."

"No, Dad. Look at me." I say it so slow, with a dry mouth, sitting up. I raise my left hand and leg as well as I can.

"You ain't no goddamned cripple," he suddenly shouts, "and I don't feel sorry for you. Or guilty about you. Maybe that's what we done too much. So you do what you have to, son. You're a man and you decide what's right and what's wrong. Now I'm going back into the kitchen, and we'll wait a few minutes. Then if you're not out, we'll hit the road back, and your mom will call you later and we'll set up your visit home like usual."

He turns to leave, and I shout for him to stay a minute longer. He looks at me. His supply of words in this environment has run out, and I can see he searches for action. He pushes my chair to the bed where I have been sitting and locks the brakes. He grabs my legs and swings them forward over the edge of the bed. I bellow to protest, but then as he is bent before me, I see the pink bald spot amidst the graying hairs on the top back of his head, that spot I have learned to concentrate on when at home he bends over to help transfer me from chair to bed, from chair to toilet, from chair to tub. Focusing on that spot allows me temporarily to escape the embarrassment of being helpless or naked in my High Line father's arms. The spot reminds me that when all the paid caregivers are left behind in the city, and my petite mother has retreated to her kitchen or front porch swing, and my brother and sister have dissolved into their own homes, there is my father, ailing back and all, squatted before me, lifting and pulling, grunting with my dead weight, never cursing as I have known him to do with a difficult chore. It may be the mothers of the world who talk on and encourage the possibilities, who offer soft words and home-baked kindnesses, but it is the fathers who uncomplainingly stoop to do the rough labor.

He gets me on my feet and pivots me to the chair. I gather myself, sit straight. My dad is a door tall and straight and rigid, but one that swings with regularity in and out. He opens and shuts on my reality.

I wheel out and smile at my family, my son, come so far to see me.

And the rockets' red glare, the loud bangs I will never again get used to, the greens and blues and violets that streak the sky, tracers of memory of past July Fourths on the High Line where you can see forever, where the horizon is always hazy when faded blue meets wheat brown, not like here now with mountains in the backdrop, dark pines lit up eerily by the lightninglike flashes of the rockets, and my mother's nails digging into the flesh of my good arm as she sits next to me in the mall parking lot, oohing and pointing as though I were a kid again on the High Line, ignoring my flinches at the loud noises, smiling at me in the gasps of light. I swear I see tears down her cheek, but maybe it's just the highlighted trails of smoke wisping in the air between us, caught like brushstrokes in silhouette across her sad smiling face. Dear Lord these are times I would welcome quick release from this earth.

John is too old for the fireworks. He stands, shifting his weight back and forth, near my father who looks as though he is standing asleep amidst the noise and crowd. John eyes the other kids his age circling around, milling through the crowd, some with cigarettes in hand: city kids to him, and he looks with longing and timidity. I surmise that anyway. I was frightened being here once as a student in the Rockies, in the city. I laugh thinking how comfortable Missoula feels now to me. I have this small advantage over my visitors.

In the morning they arrive early from their motel, packed and ready to be on the road again, stopping at the group home first to take me to breakfast. I would rather sleep in, but I force myself up and out. John and Dad struggle to transfer me into the car, and we go to Denny's.

John has been so quiet this trip, though not the sullen silences I remember. Rather he is attentive, watchful of everything I do, and I know I am greatly disappointing to him. After breakfast, we stand in the parking lot where he has wheeled me, while inside Mom visits the rest room and Dad settles the bill.

"You'll come home for Christmas, I suppose," John says. He has learned how to lead a difficult conversation.

"No," I say. "This here is home."

He looks at me and laughs. Apparently he likes my answer.

"You'll come to Gramma and Grandpa's house," he corrects himself. "Like all other Christmases. And I'll stay over a night or two while you're there, and we'll play checkers or Connect Four. We'll eat sausages and turkey sandwiches, and . . ." His voice trails off, so even though his lips are moving, there is no sound, and I'll be damned but he's crying, and I can't ever remember John crying, since I wasn't there when he was a baby, and I don't remember well anyway. I feel a pain in my heart, literally I mean. It's the saddest thing in the world to see a thirteen-year-old boy cry, because they cling so desperately to not crying, and you know they are simply out of control, and that tears them up all the worse, and you pray for them to stop, to dry those eyes, to silence the sobs and snorts because their unease threatens all of us, you know. And when it is your son who cries in front of you, for no apparent reason, other than that his father sits before him in a wheelchair, unable to speak a clear sentence, and there's little sign of any of this ever getting better, then what do you do? I've had so little training in this father business, that

I first look around for my dad, hoping he will emerge from the restaurant, to finally take this wailing boy from me. I don't know what light guides me then, but I manage to wheel close enough to John to reach around him with my good right arm and pull him down to me, so he sits in my lap and lays his head on my shoulder, and I hold him hard and close with my arm circled around him. I know I have held him when he was younger. I have seen photos of me with him in my arms, nervous relatives nearby, but I have never known such a feeling as I have now, with his head burrowed into my shoulder as his crying weakens. I will not delve into it, try to explain it. It can't be done.

I whisper to him in garbled words I'm sure he can't understand: "This is not bad; this is life. And you are a little man emerging. I love you."

When Mom and Dad come upon us, John is rising. His face is wet but stoic. He looks at me with questions in his eyes, though there is something in him that seems less sad than he was a moment before. Perhaps it has surprised him that I could comfort him.

"Mom asks about you a lot lately," he says. "She wants to be sure to see you when you come home again."

I smile as best I can.

"If you want me to, I'll see her," I say.

His grandparents urge him to get in the car. They have a ways to travel today.

When they drop me off at the group home, John says good-bye, shakes my hand like a man might do, and promises to write more than the occasional half-page note I am used to getting from him.

Before transferring me into the car, Dad tries a joke. I remember a poem which goes something like this:

Keep your eye on the ball
watch ball meet the bat
eye on the ball swing level
weight on the back foot
eye on the ball!
I dream of my father
of the long days I swing
and never miss.

16

"Robert, Robert, Robert," says Ellen.

"Ellen, Ellen," I say.

We are at a crossroads. She badgers me to recount the past, but that's not where I want to go. What is the value of revisiting pains and echoes when I am on the verge of Transitions success? She says personal history must be resolved before embarking on the future, that writing can purge the demons, and I must dig and wallow more in past sins and omissions. She demands to know about my accident, about my gradual recovery into consciousness, about my hospital and nursing home days, and it doesn't seem to matter to her that I don't remember much, and what I do remember I don't want to dwell on. But I do feel there is something vague, yet essential, that remains unexplored in my past. Something, I feel, that may be pre-injury, revolving around family, around John. I wish like hell I could remember his mother.

For you, Ellen, I could repeat the lies I've told myself about my fall. I've imagined it often as how I figure it must have been. I dream of it still on nights when I seem more restless than usual, but I know I have no accurate picture of it, or of anything about that day: just reconstructions aided by those who were last with me.

I was climbing. I was down. Those are the only things I know for sure.

Writing is reconstruction, Ellen says. How we rewrite the past is more important than what actually happened. What actually happened is lost irretrievably, and the memories only serve as jumping off points for re-created stories, altered continuously to give the illusion of meaning to the present. She may be right, I fear, but I will not live my life that way; I can't. Every day is a struggle for me to find routine and pattern and the right, appropriate actions and words. If there are none—no norms, no proper routines—then what am I struggling for? It seems a peculiar luxury for people who are not unstuck in time and place, whose memories are intact and unthreatened, to speculate about uncertainties and the absence of meanings. I must, every moment, put things in place, or at least believe places exist for things to be put.

At home, at night, in bed, I hum to myself softly, wishing for sleep, but believing I can hear from down the hallway, through shut doors, the sighings and low moanings of Lorna, fitfully trapped in her sheets, awaiting, hoping without knowing so, for another dawn. I hum in rhythm with what I imagine to be her breath till I am rocked into my fantasies. I am so sleepy the story line is not stable, and Lorna's face changes into Jodi's and back again. And this hybrid woman and I walk on reliable legs to a barn, my uncle's barn on the High Line. We climb a ladder to the hayloft, we undress and caress, and it is all so gentle and loving and beautiful. Is there a real memory here mingling with my imagining? Whatever. We become divine.

The fantasy though is out of control, intruded upon by images of rolling and falling from the loft. I am alone then, feeling like a yo-yo, rising and falling, never staying up or down for long. I am played out, I yell, I wish only for an elusive rest. I feel grabbed by a large invisible hand which at once is soft and comforting, yet tight and restraining, and continues with the up and down motion. As best I can, I hollow out my brain, try to sew up the seams so no images can break in, so I will be completely blank and finally, finally at rest. But the images come nonstop, of Lorna, of Jodi, of John, of Brett, of Jennifer, of Ellen, of my father, laughing. Then I am in the barn, in the hay, and the hay is an orange-red color, like Indian paintbrush. The hay swallows me, then like a volcano erupting, spits me out, tumbling me out of the loft, tumbling me a long way before I land, rudely, yet in one piece, on the bare planks of the wooden floor.

As I write this I know I am re-creating, even redreaming on the spot, changing the contents of the original dream. And it bothers me greatly, though I believe I am being true to the spirit of my dreams.

I pray God to hold me till the world is still, or till I find the quiet axis on which the world spins.

I am not in any kind of mood to be wakened in the morning, and I am surly with staff, who never seem to understand we disabled can have a bad day. As though this day is no different from days when I have had a full night's sleep, I am hustled from bed to breakfast to van to Transitions. I am pushed hard all day, lectured at for not trying, for yawning during sessions. When I finally am home again, I fall asleep before dinner in my chair while watching TV.

At dinner, I am minimally revived, and I sit next to Lorna. We have been distant since my last unsuccessful encounter with her, and I wonder if she misses me. When I am able to focus on her and think about her, I feel guilty, that I am abandoning her somehow. I promise myself to be more attentive and wish I could help with her feeding as I used to, but she is all tubes now, with nurses coming daily. I interrupt my own eating to force my bad left hand to pat her hand, and I smile at her. Her eyes seem to show appreciation for the gesture.

After dinner, Lorna is wheeled to her room and put to bed. I sit with her; Jennifer props the door open and keeps watch. I cannot say anything, though Lorna chants occasionally: "Definitely. Definitely."

Finally I find words.

"Lorna, I apologize," I say, though I'm not sure for what. It feels like I have much to be sorry for. "I should have been more . . . ," I say but can't finish the thought. More what?

I wheel as near as I can, reach and caress her sweaty brow. Behind me I hear Jennifer shuffle, alert for any misbehavior. I turn to Jennifer and ask as clearly as I can, "Please, help me stand."

I have to repeat a couple times, and when she finally understands, she eyes me with suspicion.

"Please," I beg, "for a second, let me stand."

Jennifer undoes my seat belt, locks my brakes, gets behind me, and helps me till I am somewhat stable before Lorna.

"Now," I say, "I want to kiss Lorna's forehead."

Again Jennifer looks unsure of me, and she studies my eyes. Then she sits on the bed, still holding onto my waist. She positions herself so that I can bend slowly into her and Lorna, while staying steady and not falling. Slowly, slowly I lean my weight into Jennifer, closer and closer to Lorna. Then I am there; my lips brush Lorna's forehead, my nose is tickled by wisps of her hair. As I rise, Lorna's eyelids flicker, a smile comes to her face, her lips move. "Definitely," she may be saying. Jennifer lowers me to my chair and pushes me back. I sit for a while till I am sure Lorna is back asleep, peacefully, then wheel myself quietly out.

I find Jennifer in the kitchen, finishing the dishes, and I offer my help in cleaning up. After all, I am learning such skills at Transitions. She smiles and gives me a broom.

"Thank you," I say, "for your help."

"No problem," she says, then adds, "I can't remember you ever thanking me before."

I sweep what dirt I can. When I've collected a pile, Jennifer holds the dustpan for me. I try not to but can't help noticing her hair, blonde highlights shimmering in the fluorescent light of the kitchen; her breasts when she leans down push at the worn shiny threads of her green cotton blouse. I sense she may be lost and sad till she lifts her head, stands straight, looks in my eyes, and smiles yet again. I duck my head, turn and wheel down the hallway, past Lorna's dimly lit room, to my room, where I will try again to conquer my fitfulness, to drift with my thoughts into sleep.

17

With our knees nearly touching, Doctor Larry sits opposite me, ramrod straight, a slightly overweight man who likes to fiddle with his tie when he's thinking. He sweats a lot, but then summer's in full bloom.

"There seems to be progress," he says, drawing out the words longer than necessary. "No major outbursts lately that I've heard of. How are you feeling about things here or at home?"

Doctor Larry is okay; he tries. But I'm not in the mood to focus today, to try to recall incidents I can't remember. I grunt to him I'm fine and hope he leaves it at that.

But he's not paid to leave things alone.

"You don't seem very happy today. Are you tired? Upset? Anything I can help with?"

"Just a bad day. Nothing particular."

"How's your friend at the group home? The woman with MS?"

"Lorna," I say, perversely happy I get a turn to help someone with a name they can't remember. "She's doing great. Getting a lot of rest. I think she and I will go to dinner tomorrow night."

"I see," he says, but his eyes show he doesn't believe me.

"Lorna and I went walking yesterday around the mall. We got ice cream and cake, and we won a prize at the arcade. We won two-hundred-and-two tickets from playing skeeball and could choose anything we wanted."

"What did you choose?"

"I don't remember. A lion, I think. A huge stuffed lion."

"I'm glad to hear Lorna is feeling better," he says. "She must have made quite a recovery."

"Yeah," I say, feeling lost, getting unstuck, knowing I'm not quite telling the truth, but still I can visualize the events I describe. Somehow, somewhere, I know they've happened. Haven't they?

"Are you sure this all happened yesterday?" Doctor Larry waits for my answer, fiddling with his tie, sweat beading around his collar. I say nothing.

After skeeball, Lorna and I go to the J. C. Penney's, and we pick out a perfect yellow sundress, the yellow of sunflower petals spread wide to the heat and light. She tries it on and emerges from the dressing room for me tall and bright as a sunflower, my flower smiling and twirling so the edges of the dress curl up and dance around her brown thighs.

"Robert," Doctor Larry interrupts my thoughts and grabs my hand. "We need to continue our work together on distinguishing between reality and fantasy. Remember: fantasies are fine as long as you know the difference between them and reality. It takes a lot of effort for you, but you've got to keep trying."

"I'm fine," I say. "Can I go now?"

"I don't mind your fantasies," he says, ignoring my question. "We all need our escapes now and then. But don't run completely from the real world."

"My real life," I chuckle. "That's what my mom calls my life before I was hurt."

"Now is your real life, Robert. Confront it. Live with it. See the women and men around you as real people."

"What am I?" I bellow the question, and repeat it even louder when I see Doctor Larry hasn't understood. I am astounded. I don't know where the question comes from or what it means, yet it feels essential.

"What am I?" I repeat. "To you, for instance? A client, a patient? Someone who needs assistance? A riddle to be figured out so you can say you've earned your paycheck? Do you know me?"

"Yes," Doctor Larry lies through his teeth. "Yes, I know you."

"There's staff always around me following the treatment plan," I say. "I feel I'm always in a corner, alone, an object of pity or help."

“This is good, Robert,” Doctor Larry says. “Go with your feelings.”

I stare at him, wanting to cry, but that would be too daring a breakdown, too much of a connection between us. He bears down on a tablet on his desk, furiously scribbling notes, then studies me, fiddles with his tie again.

“So Robert, are you angry with your caregivers? Let it out so we can deal with it.”

I don’t give him an answer, but think: no, it’s not anger. More sadness. Disappointment. Loneliness.

Then he asks peculiar questions, a barrage that silences me: “What do you think of your caregivers? Are they just paid staff to you? What am I to you, just a parasite, taking money to listen to you without caring? What is Jodi? Just an object of your fantasies? Robert, what is Lorna to you?”

Then I lower my head, because that’s how I concentrate, ridding myself of as many distractions as possible, but his questions are too complicated, too abstract for me to keep in focus. I hear the scratching of his pen on paper, the hum of an air conditioner, voices and footsteps in the hallway. With relief, I surrender to the stimuli around me and give up the mental concentration. When he realizes I will not answer, Doctor Larry tells me our time is up.

Brett gathers me outside the door, and I make him write down the good doctor’s questions for future pondering.

18

At Transitions, when their backs are turned, I steal away. They won't be happy. They'll write me up in their books. They'll tell Doctor Larry, and Jodi, and director Clare. But how do I explain? The need to escape. To pretend my independence.

They are right, I guess, though I will never admit it. I'm not safe on my own. How quickly I am lost in the hospital corridor maze embarrasses me. I wave off offers of help from nurses and staff who must see I'm out of place and don't know where I belong. I keep on wheeling.

This is what one does, you know, on well-oiled wheels down quiet polished floors, no squeaks, no bounces, no sudden jolts. Just the sound of my breathing, the occasional grunts as I push along, the whoosh of fabric when people walk past.

I am wheeling down a side hallway of bright colors, of trees and jungle animals on the walls. A zebra swishes its black-and-white tail, a lion fluffs its mane, a giraffe cranes and smiles in giraffe-bemused fashion at me, all bizarre figures nailed to the hallway walls. And strangest of all, before me at the dead end of the hall, where you must make a turn through double swinging doors, is a life-size wooden merry-go-round horse, golden-coated with white mane and tail, a copper-colored saddle with green and red trim, and a golden post running from the floor through its middle, spearing the air above it. The horse's mouth is open, lips flared and teeth showing, as though smiling or grimacing. In its saddle, leaning against the golden pole, sits a large sky-blue teddy bear. My God, what have we here? For a moment, I wonder at what hallucinations my brain may be producing. Have I finally become unstuck totally in time and place, my brain divorced from reality as you know it?

At a large window in one wall, between monkeys and antelope, five or six people gather, and I wheel to them, and they part, as though my chair gives me the right to be in the front row. On the other side of the window, in tiny metal cribs, two babies peer up at the new world, wiggling and crying and protesting, while the strangers on my side of the glass point and smile and laugh. I do not see the babies as all that happy, despite the crowd's efforts. Their cries are muffled behind the glass as their loving relatives beam, oblivious to the fear and pain.

The head-injured, I am told, wake from their comas like this, like angry babies. For weeks we curse uncontrollably at family and staff, flail at whoever comes near. Yell and cry like wild beasts. My mother says out of the coma I was like a newborn. After I settled a bit, she had to teach me everything all over again: to walk and talk and tie my shoes. It upsets me that she speaks with a note of fondness of those mothering days, because there is something about the rebirth we head-injured like to resist.

The babies are much too sad for me to watch anymore. Or maybe, it is the reaction of the relatives that revolts me, so smiling, so satisfied, so sure all this is fine and good, this entry into the world where . . . where things are not always so fine and appropriate. I put my good foot down and propel myself away as fast as I can. Out of the hallway, past the jungle animals who stick out from the wall, who look too goofy, too happy to be real.

I'm panicked. And the panic is all the worse because I can't run or wheel with any kind of speed. Whatever I do must be done with a slowness that contradicts my fear. God, my breaths are labored, deep and pained. They fog my mind, slip me into a kind of trance where I'm more comfortable, where I don't notice time or distance so much or the people around me. I used to not be able to remember even a whisper of those early days, of reentry to the world, and now what I remember I realize are only re-creations of scenes based on others' recollections; such is the frailty of memory, too easily disturbed and too easily influenced. Can I believe the fantastic stories they tell me of my rage, of my fierceness upon awakening? Did my mother really lie in bed with me and sing me lullabies, kneel on her broken knees, her wiry hair bent before me, to fasten my feet to footrests? These are the stories now, the photos of our mental family album.

An elevator door whooshes open near me and I pause, the noise oddly breaking my panic, giving me a thing to focus on outside my head. I sit and wait, watch the buttons by the door light up, till finally the door whooshes open again and a nurse walks out and I wheel in. The door closes, and I am alone inside the cubicle. I am ridiculously impressed by my actions, by my dash into this elevator car, by my whole flight from Transitions. I'm too excited to think which button I might want to push, how far I might want to ascend. The elevator just takes off then, by itself, going up. When it stops, I am not sure I want off, but an orderly-type person guesses this is my floor and that I need help, so he pushes me out. My attempts at protest are not understood, and there I am outside in a hall as the silver elevator doors swoosh shut, coldly and efficiently.

Okay. Down a long hallway I wheel, bump through doors, till I am stopped by a smell that resonates in my brain as threatening, though I don't know why.

It is quiet in a way hard to describe. The regular hospital sounds are there: rattling trays and carts, low professional voices, hurried footsteps, doors opening and shutting, codes announced over the public address. Yet it's almost like these sounds don't exist; there is nothing but silence here, like the silence of a church between services, a hushed waiting, but not nearly as sacred.

I wheel on, feeling like Dorothy and Scarecrow in the forest, wide-eyed and cautious. I peer into rooms, where mostly I see only drawn curtains, though occasionally I spy feet at the end of a bed or a patient sitting up or a nurse bending over. There are moans, soft words,, television sounds. The professionals' official bustle contrasts with the stillness of patients in their beds. One woman sits on the side of her bed, bare legs and feet dangling, not quite reaching the floor. She looks right at me, yet I know she doesn't see me. She is skinny, old, white-skinned and blue-veined, and has hollowed-out black eyes. Her lips are thin and purple; her body curves like the neck of a swan; her arms are straight, her hands stationed on the mattress, balancing her. Then I notice the tubes in and out of her arm and chest. She seems now to see me, though I don't know how I sense that since nothing about her face or posture changes, except maybe some awareness in the eyes. Temporarily she is a pronghorn at a water hole, feeling a mountain lion near, looking round, sizing up the approaches, the escape routes. But just as quickly the look shuts down; her face contorts, then relaxes. Her guard is down and she lets loose a sigh that rises from deep inside, or maybe from below her, from the depths of the hospital itself. In our quiet, her sigh is like a loud bleat surrounding me with such pain and fear I can't move. She sighs again, and I struggle to avoid being swallowed by the sound, or by her eyes, so hollowed they create a whirlpool that would suck me in. An aide brushes past me into the room, closes the curtain, cuts off my sight, and I know I have escaped something.

I retreat and again wheel as fast as I can, to nowhere. I want the elevator but can't find it. Nothing looks familiar; the halls remain so awfully quiet, and I am afraid and ashamed to ask for help. I see a bright red exit sign and wheel towards it, but when I get there find only stairs. A nurse asks if I need help, but I turn and wheel from her. She persists, easily keeping pace with me. "Please, let me help you. You look so lost."

But I'm not lost, I think. Just temporarily misplaced. I can find my own way. Leave me alone and let me think . . .

Okay. Give me a clue. What floor am I on? Oh, don't go on too much, woman. She babbles on, trying to get me to respond, with pity enough to disgust me. Her pity won't allow her to be quiet and try to understand my garbled speech. She reminds me of my mother and her talk about my lost real life, of the real life she still believes I will one day miraculously return to. And then what, Mom? Will I be in college again? Will I be playing Carnegie Hall? Since we're talking miracles here, will we retrieve the lost years too? Will you be as young as you were? Or will we not both be as close to death as we really are?

"What's your name? Where do you want to go?" The nurse will not relent, so finally I stop and sit straight and swallow. I speak loudly and slowly, as clear as I can. I ask for the elevator, and I think she understands. She pushes me to the silver doors, enters with me, and asks which floor. I reach myself and push the button for the bottom floor. I want to go back to Transitions now. One can take only so much adventure before home starts to look good again. She glances at her watch, gives me an anxious look, then leaps out just before the doors close. I am alone again.

On the bottom floor, I wander. I don't remember all my travels, but somehow I end up in the hospital recreation room, at the piano where Brett once listened to me play. I push my left hand down hard onto a tabletop, prying the fingers till they separate a little, and I begin to pound the keys. Though I've been told my left hand has stopped making progress, I think I am able to spread it farther than before, so my fingers can leap more than one key at a time. I bang out my improvisations of old Christmas songs, then hurl myself into what I remember of a Chopin mazurka. My left hand starts to seriously cramp, my eyes tear up, but I will not quit. I bang mercilessly, tunelessly, on the piano. I don't know what others hear, but I feel lost in the rhythm, in the jangled music I create of hallways and jungles, of birth and dying. It feels I have had too short a time alone when Brett comes from behind, pulls me away, and harshly lectures me about leaving on my own.

Yes, yes, whatever you say, my dear Brett. But have you ever wheeled so far as I?

19

Weeks have misted by. August heat whispers around the bend, as the ends of my mustache soddenly wilt into the corners of my mouth. To remember much about the passage of time, I study my memory book, and there I find staff and I have written that progress has been good. With the exception of my escape through the halls of the hospital, I have committed no serious breaches of rules or etiquette. And I have been upright more often, successfully handling my modified walker, and ambulating slowly down Transitions halls with Brett next to me, holding onto the back of my gait belt. The wheelchair remains, and will remain, I'm told, for independent traveling. I will never walk alone.

I read too how I've made a bologna sandwich without help from Brett or anyone else. I'm also using a microwave with staff cues and folding my laundry and putting my clothes away with minimal reminders. Brett jokes (he's written it in my memory book) that Transitions will make me a perfect wife for someone.

So today we have this review conference, and much of staff is here, including Brett and Clare and Tonya and Doctor Larry. And Jodi is here and Jennifer from the group home, and I read to them about how I've progressed.

"Robert's been good as gold at home," Jennifer says, smiling at me. "He's been doing the chores around the house you folks have suggested. He hasn't gotten into any trouble. He's been appropriate with staff and with Lorna too."

"Appropriate." Has there ever been a more evil-sounding word? They have run "normal" right out of the dictionary and replaced it with "appropriate," as though that is any less judgmental. So yes, Transitions staff says, one by one, Robert is appropriate. I should be smiling (and God knows, maybe I am), since appropriate means progress, means steps towards independence, etc. I tape the meeting so I will have what they say verbatim. Tonya tells the team: "Robert has been walking with a walker and standby assistance every day. His transfers have improved minimally, and I continue to recommend at least standby assist. He's been successfully using a footrest for his left foot, which has improved his posture. Since the operation, his left hand has shown a great deal more flexibility. Robert reports no pain from contracture, and he's been very consistent with exercises to open up the hand with very little prompting from staff. However the hand has opened as much as it will. I don't foresee any further progress."

The speech therapist says, "Robert has been entirely appropriate the last few weeks. Use of the footrest has helped him to sit up straighter, which has, in turn, helped improve his breathing, swallowing, and his speech. He has become more intelligible since coming here, but still requires cues to sit up straight, slow down, and swallow before speaking. He has slowed down while eating, so he is safer. I still recommend he avoid nuts and raw vegetables that are hard to chew. Cognitively, Robert's been using his memory book consistently to remember events and keep pace with his schedule. He requires assistance to write in the book and to find the section he needs. He needs occasional cues to use the book. He has improved on a computer keyboard, and a word processor works much better for him than writing."

La la la la la la . . .

Words rain on me. I catch on what's important. As they speak about my hand, I force it down and open on the tabletop, proving there's continued progress, that I will be back to my preinjury piano-playing one of these days if I just keep pressing, if I keep working the hand. Rehab staff nod at me reassuringly with smiles, and I nod back. This is, according to Jodi, a very favorable meeting.

Doctor Larry reports (and I quote): "In our dyad sessions, Robert is achieving satisfactory progress in maximizing his optimal potential . . ." which roughly translates into: "I've been a good boy, usually willing to talk about what's bothering me."

Testing has shown my memory is not as bad as I often display. Generally, I have average recall of things preinjury, and my short-term memory, though not nearly as good as the average person's, is better than I pretend. Doctor Larry says, "Robert seems to have selective memory gaps. Some of what he says he doesn't remember are things he chooses not to remember—or perhaps his subconscious blocks from him."

The people around the table laugh and kid me about this. They say they've seen me choose not to remember times when I've been inappropriate. Judging by their relieved smiles, I suppose it makes them feel better to believe I can manipulate my memory use somewhat. I laugh with them, an appropriately guilty look on my face, though to be honest, I'm not sure what they all see as so funny.

"For instance," Doctor Larry says, "Robert will remember a few pretty exact details about my last meeting with him, what we talked about, even what I was wearing, but always there seems to be a few things he represses—or for some reason, can't keep stored in his memory."

Brett adds, "Like he claims he can't remember a thing about his escape and trip through the hospital, yet he can tell me what song he was playing on the piano when I finally found him."

"Yes," Doctor Larry says. "It amazes me the details he can give of his home on the High Line, yet then struggle for a description of his son, and can't recall key names, like the mother of his son."

"So what?" I roar, then calm down immediately, remembering to be appropriate. "Why are you bringing this up?" I say, speaking as clearly as possible, and I can see most people understand me.

"Occasional details of his memories," Doctor Larry says, ignoring me, "may be re-creations, or fabrications. Robert has a rich fantasy life."

"What did you say about my son? That I can't recognize him? That's not true."

Finally Doctor Larry turns to me. "I think you do quite well with your son and your family. I brought it up just as an example of your peculiar lapses in memory. I wonder if those lapses mean there's more for you to explore in those areas. I would like to spend more time talking with you about your family and your past."

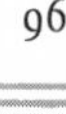

"I want to work on stuff that's happening now," I say. "What do I need to do today?"

Doctor Larry turns from me and addresses the rest of the group around the table: "Robert doesn't always distinguish well between his fantasies and reality. I believe this is more a result of his brain injury than a psychiatric condition. It's not a major problem until we get to safety issues."

"Yes, we all have lingering concerns about that," Clare the director says, and I feel a consensus "tsk, tsk" aimed from all sides. "Though over the last couple weeks, Robert has certainly been appropriate" (and they all grin and sigh on that word), "he continues to demonstrate problems with insight and judgment."

"That complicates plans," Jodi says, "to move him into a more independent place in the community. Doctor, can we do more to orient Robert to reality?"

"I'm not crazy," I say.

"No one says you are," Jodi quickly assures me.

"Don't we all have a fantasy life?" Jennifer, who has been silent all this time, speaks. "When I confront Robert, I think he's able to tell what's going on at home and what's just in his head."

"He likes to retreat," Doctor Larry says.

"And don't you too," Jennifer asks, "when reality gets too harsh?"

"Of course," Doctor Larry says. "But what we're talking about is considering giving him more freedom in the community, not having staff around twenty-four hours a day. I'm concerned about how his fantasies affect his judgment. I'm not sure how safe Robert is by himself."

"Just how independent would he be outside the group home?" Clare asks Jodi.

"If we can find the right roommate for him—one who needs a similar level of services—they can share caregivers. And Robert would continue at his day program Monday through Friday. We'd be able to provide nearly continuous coverage every day, and we'd have an on-call system at night so he could call for help at any time."

“But would he call appropriately? Would he call when he needed help?” Clare asks.

“He’d definitely be safer in the group home,” Jodi says.

“What’s happening?” I say. Jennifer puts her hand on my arm, pats me.

“If you want him focusing more on reality,” Jennifer says, “give him a reason to stay focused. Give him new possibilities. Real things of importance. Of course he nods out now. Because every day’s the same, and he’s got people to do everything for him, so it doesn’t matter if he screws up or not, if he makes a wrong choice, or if he doesn’t do what he’s supposed to. Somebody is always there to rescue him.”

“You make a good point,” Doctor Larry says. “But safety . . .”

“When is it his choice?” Jennifer interrupts. “Can’t he choose what risks he wants to take? Life isn’t secure for any of us.”

“She’s right,” Jodi says. “The whole point of Transitions was to prepare him for a more independent life. And if a trial out in the community fails, he can always move back to the group home.” She rises and walks over to me, squats in front of me, steadies herself with a hand on my chair’s armrest.

“We need to find you an accessible apartment,” Jodi says, smiling. “And a roommate. What do you say? Do you want to work on this? Is this what you want?”

I pause before answering. I pause in the pools of her eyes which genuinely seem to sparkle, which seem to invite me to new deep worlds, which promise me safety and security. I try to imagine apartment life(my own kitchen, my TV, my table, my chairs. Fear slices through me that I will be abandoned, I will be lonely, I will do something crazy and idiotic while alone. I will transfer by myself and break a bone. Or I will wheel out to the nearest bar, drink myself silly, invite patrons home to party. I will be beat up, left for dead. How incredible, I marvel, after so many years of being taken care of, that I am so terrified at the prospect of independence. I am ashamed of my fears and shake my head violently. I look at Jodi and the surprise that registers in her face makes me realize she takes my head-shaking as a refusal of her offer. I quickly change my head’s direction and nod, and smile and say, “Yes, yes. I want to try it. I want to try it.” Then annoyingly enough, images of Lorna cross my brain, and I am sad. Can I leave her? It's not fair, a voice screams inside me, that she should be left behind. It's too late now to say anything different. Jodi has heard my acceptance. She has sat down again and speaks excitedly with Jennifer, and then with Transitions staff. Brett too is smiling, looking at me. He extends a hand for me to shake. "We'll make the changes as smooth as possible," he says. "Congratulations, Robert."

The room is filled with excitement, even as the meeting settles back into routine. Staff talk one on one about what I will need for apartment life, what yet they can work on with me. They speak about accessibility, about my getting special utensils to help with meal preparation, about needing furniture, about what qualities a good roommate would have.

But for me, Lorna haunts my mind so I am useless for the rest of the meeting. I know with a word I could end all this talk. I could say I want to stay where I am. I could say I'm scared, or I could say I don't want to abandon Lorna. I need give no explanation. Finally something rises in me that blots out images of Lorna, something strong and vital like the blood that runs through my veins. I will not give her up, I think. I will stay true. But I will lose this opportunity. And the voice that has gathered within me whispers a dirty secret to me that I fight against but lose. Lorna may not even recognize my absence. Lorna is dying, and I am living. I will have to let Lorna go sooner, not later.

I am immensely sad. Talk of independence makes me so.

20

Sunday A.M.

Can Lorna go to church with me?

No, she's too sick.

Is there no end of this for her?

Not till the final end.

It sucks.

Yes.

I travel the hall—my bedroom to kitchen, past her room, no joy singing in my wheels, no blessings afoot for the lady of my life. She barely stirs, she lies still, her breaths barely raising the blankets, her voice reduced to low groans this morning.

Is she getting worse?

Always.

Will she stay here or go to a nursing home?

We hope she stays here.

More people than usual have been coming for Lorna, beyond the regular parade of staff and family. Hospice people who help you die. Nurses and counselors who not only relieve staff but also talk to us other residents, who take the family aside and speak in whispers, occasional laughs, and tears.

Ellen suggests I write more of this. She sits in her chair, legs crossed, the computer on the desk to the side of us, as I have taken a break from my writing. Where am I now? Not at the group home anymore. Transitions? The day program? Neither seems right. I have

Ellen sitting here, clicking her tongue, trying to coax me past the break in my writing, and it all feels odd and out of place, which may be why I can't remember details of it well, and maybe it doesn't even happen today at all.

"Write," Ellen says. "Get this out."

"You know how I need my breaks," I tell her. "You've never bothered me when I've stopped before."

"You've never stopped in the middle of an issue before. You need to explore."

"To hell with you."

Let me explain, faithful reader (Ellen says, "Good; explanations are necessary"). I am not at the group home. It is not really Sunday A.M. I am in Transitions at my computer with Ellen, reconstructing the past week's events. I am taking a break, because my fingers ache.

"Liar," says Ellen.

Why oh why is she so difficult today? "Here," I say to her, "is my keyboard. Perhaps you'd like to type out an explanation for your odd behavior."

She laughs. "You write," she says.

I go to church

wq;oafjq';woekbv;'

Hah, Ellen bangs on my keyboard. "No," she insists. "You are not at church yet. You are with Lorna."

"Lorna's dying," I say. "Lorna's dead. I go on."

"That easily?"

"Bastard," I say. "I must get to church. Lorna will be here when I get back."

"Are you so sure?"

It's a big day for me. After church, Brett is due to make a rare Sunday appearance as I've finally rated a weekend visit from this nine-to-five Monday-through-Friday guy. We have an apartment or two to look at.

"You would leave Lorna behind."

"Look at all the people visiting her now, sitting with her. There's barely time I can be there alone with her. It's over. I've been good to her. I have nothing to be guilty about."

"I agree," says Ellen. "I'm just not convinced you believe that yourself."

"Have you become psychologist now, as well as writing tutor?"

"One of a writer's biggest weaknesses is failing to push hard enough on things that matter most."

Okay, okay. Lorna dying. Lorna dead. Lorna dead.

Today it doesn't register. Today I want only to deny it, to run away, and take care of myself. Am I not allowed? Can I not just let this be for now? Allow it to percolate in my brain till it becomes clearer?

I wheel to Lorna, park beside the hospice staff nurse who weakly grins at me and touches my forearm in a weak show of sympathy. I can't hear anything in this room, not even Lorna's breathing. Her face has thinned and whitened. If I were able, I'd rip all these tubes and plastic bags from her. I might smother her with her own pillow. It is something a head-injured person might be allowed to get away with. After all, we have no control, you know, no judgment about what is and what is not appropriate. Why do they prolong this? Why this somber death watch? Is this the reality they all want me to concentrate on? My fantasies are more humane.

A bead of sweat—or perhaps it's a wandering tear—slides down the side of Lorna's cheek. Her eyelids flutter and open, and she speaks in gasps only folks experienced with her can interpret. "Definitely," she says, "definitely."

Okay Ellen. Okay all ye mighty therapists and counselors, ye staff of all the worlds. Okay, I stare into the face of reality, there in Lorna, the pale, skinny, and bony emanations of her cheekbones wet with sweat and tears, her body barely a low hill under the covers. And if I could raise my eyes to the mirror that hangs on her closet door, I would see my well-fed ruddy face, mouth misshapen with a left lip droop, moist with drool, my eyes never quite properly open, my hair disheveled, and I know I probably haven't shaved today. And I am the lucky one, the one who lives and moves on. This is reality.

In a week, in a month, someone else will occupy her bed, some other suffering person will be here in place of Lorna, who will instead lie somewhere underground. I will not visit her then. I will not mourn her passing because I have my own frail life to lead, and what was she anyway to me but a chance encounter? I assure you if I had not fallen and broken my brain I would never have met her, and if I had seen her in a park or downtown wheeled by a caregiver, I would have looked away without a thought of how lucky I am to be whole and alive and upright and independent and walking. But wait, I have to say my years of disability have taught me one thing: you un-disabled people are not any luckier than we who wheel past your averted eyes. Your trials and your capabilities are different, but we have seen life through totally different lenses, and though I don't claim any more strength of insight from my predicament, neither do I admit to being any less than you.

Lorna will die. Just sooner than most of us. Is there some grace here I refuse to acknowledge? Were we destined to meet? Have I gained anything through her? Or did I just use her to pass the time? To make time more bearable? Had I not fallen, I would have pursued other dreams, other women. Maybe, God knows, I would be married to Jodi now with our 2.2 kids trekking in our minivan through our suburban paradise. Or maybe I would still be on the High Line, pitching hay and stepping through cow shit, getting drunk on Friday nights at the corner bar, coming home late to . . . what's her name? John's mother. Maybe I would be back East, a concert pianist, a la-de-da musician in the Boston orchestra, sipping cocktails after a performance, la-de-da-ing with the fans, with fellow musicians, speaking in unbearable accents. Maybe I would . . .

I have escaped reality for a minute here. Thank you, Ellen, for suffering the diversion. I think our reality needs a turn or two into fantasy.

From her bed, Lorna looks at me with dull eyes that carry no recognition. I wipe the wetness from her face with my big clumsy damaged hand.

Jesus Jesus Jesus Jesus Jesus, I say.

Shall we gather by the river
the beautiful the beautiful river

So the church bellows, and I sing more boisterously, more desperately, than ever. The old ladies show me grins so wide and sweet you imagine them in perpetual indulgent smile, beyond the need for swallowing, or taking any breath from this less-than-perfect airspace between us. Unfortunately, the younger congregation members, who are no more pious than their elders, but more anxious for perfect spiritual experience, frown and wag their heads in my direction. One even has the gall to ask me to sing quieter, and Jennifer, who accompanies me today, squeezes my arm and whispers for me to take a break.

Not today, methinks. Let my poor fellow churchgoers find nunneries and monasteries if they want quiet. I must bellow today—and maybe tomorrow—maybe beyond that. I can't control myself, I tell Jennifer.

"The beautiful the beautiful river, milk and honey on the other side, coming forth to carry me home . . ."

The singing forces images of happier times with Lorna into my head, films over my worries, allows temporary calm. In the pauses of relative quiet, I remind myself how Brett will meet me after church. I focus on that thought, but when the singing resumes, images of Lorna sneak into my mind. Suddenly, I feel her fill every part of me, radiating from my chest into the extremities, passing life into damaged fingers and toes. What miracle is this? No matter. It is quickly come and quickly gone. The service is over.

"Thank you, Robert," the minister says at the back door after church. "You were quite enthusiastic today."

"Fine," I say and pull on Jennifer to hurry, to get me to the van. I am anxious to get to the apartment where we will meet Brett, where everyday reality will relieve me of the mysteries and desperation of faith.

Let me tell you what I thought of the apartment. Jennifer and I drive to a complex (no jokes please) where first-floor apartments are accessible for wheelchairs. Brett helps me inspect Apartment 112, a bedroom each for me and a roommate (identity yet to be determined). The closets have low shelves and dowels at a level where I can hang clothes myself. The kitchen has a raised sink and raised stove-top burners so my wheelchair can fit under them. The bathroom has plenty of space, with strategically placed grab bars and a roll-in shower. All state-of-the-art accessibility.

"How do you like it?" Brett asks with a tone in his voice that indicates how pleased he is to show me this promising place. Jennifer crowds next to him, both now in front of me, obscuring my view of Formica countertops, of gleaming white linoleum, of hunter green bathroom tiles. I nod and grunt a yes, and they believe me content.

They part and I wheel into the bathroom, where it takes me a minute to realize something vital is missing.

"I want a tub," I say. Brett is in the hall, commenting on the living room where the carpet is sturdy and attractive, but low enough to allow a wheelchair an easy ride. Jennifer hears me, and I see a worried, exasperated look cross her face.

"Not many folks are lucky enough to have a roll-in shower," she says.

"I hate showers."

When Brett joins us in the bathroom, Jennifer says, "He wants a tub."

"But this apartment is perfect," Brett says. "It'll be a long time before a place like this is available again."

"I would die if I can't take a bath."

"But a roll-in shower would make things so much easier for you. You could be mostly independent in a shower like this."

"I'm independent in a bath."

"You need help transferring in and out," Jennifer says, then smiles weakly at Brett. "Robert does love his baths. He'd spend hours in a tub if we let him."

"It's my private time," I say.

"But what about the other advantages?" Brett asks. "The accessible sink and stove and closets. Aren't they a good trade-off for the lack of a tub?"

"I want a tub."

Brett shakes his head and rubs his hand over the back of his neck. "Well," he says, "we could put a tub in here, but I've never made a place *less* accessible before. No, we can't do it. Robert, I really think you should at least try this place."

He looks forlorn, hurt that I might reject his efforts on my behalf. He sighs as Jennifer steps behind me, leans down and asks quietly if I might want to look at the living room more closely.

"I can envision you here, Robert. Perfect place for you."

Jennifer pushes me past Brett; my wheels whisper onto the carpet. There is a large window in front of me, with a view of more cadet gray apartment buildings. Between them I can glimpse green grass and the banks of the Clark Fork River. And then I see Brett's reflection in the glass as he stands behind me.

“It’s your choice,” he says. “We can look for another place.” His voice carries a sad weight in it. Why, I wonder, is he so dejected? He won’t have to live here. In fact, once I’m settled, I’ll be done with Transitions, and Brett will be done with me. So I’m led to believe.

“Come on,” Brett says. “Try this apartment. Trust me, you’d be stupid not to take it. This would set up a great transition for you.”

Stupid. I would be stupid. I would choose against something a rational normal person would never choose against. I feel already the shame, the talk behind my back, how that stupid head-injured Robert made such a dumb choice.

“What if I move in and then don’t like it here?” I ask.

“If you don’t like it, we can look for another place. You won’t be stuck here the rest of your life.”

“It’s not that easy,” Jennifer says, joining the conversation, “to move again, to find a place. The whole bit.”

“It’s not impossible,” Brett says.

“I suppose I could try it,” I say.

“Do what you want,” Jennifer says. “Choose what you think is right for you.”

“Yeah, yeah,” I mutter and back away from both of them, not understanding what I’m feeling, wanting them both mostly just to shut up. I’m overwhelmed by the thought of all this change, of such a decision thrust in my lap. Me, who has had everything scheduled for him, day and night, asked now for a decision of such high magnitude. And what is right for me? God knows, and He ain’t telling. I want my tub, but the place is fully accessible. I have to be careful with this decision. I don’t want to be less-than-smart.

“Okay,” I say, out of frustration, out of a fear that I can’t possibly face Brett’s exasperation or condescension. “Maybe I’ll like showers.”

“Great,” says Brett. “We’ll have a fun time decorating. What about the kitchen table in that corner?”

Oh God, I sigh. Do the choices never end?

21

My Keyboard Has Lost the Letter " "

A man's home is his _astle.
Unless like me, he has aides
and attendants
and _aregivers
and therapists
and _ase managers
who have swum the moat,
so to speak,
daily invade my inner san_tum
to monitor my shits,
my goings and _omings,
my habits of all sorts
I fear I will always have
too many lords and ladies
up these _astle walls.

Hah, Ellen finds my letter "c" and we are happy once again. Just thrilled I can again type out the word "aCCess," and "CaCkle," and better yet, "CaCophony" and "CirCumCise." However, in the meantime, I have stumbled upon the awful truth that the letter "c" is wholly dispensable. After all, we have "s" and "k" available, who are, I imagine, quite kapable and in no need of a bak-up letter for their sounds. "C" is a poor kousin in the alphabet, a weaker version of better letters. Why have we put up with "c" for so long? Katered to him? Allowed him existense? Would our lives not be easier without him, less entangled? Why do we not simply do away with him, banish him from our spase? Without him, spelling would be easier and the word "quik" would be quiker. After all, who deklared that we must be married to him, for better or worse, for ri_her, for poorer?

Damn, it appears we will never be "ri_h" without him.

Okay, I'm funning you all. I'm taking advantage of a natural crisis wherein my keyboard had lost its "c," but now Ellen has kindly fixed the stuck key and she begs me to stop this nonsense. So "c" has returned, and I share it with you: Big C, little c, even the seven C's: C C C C C C C.

Not so much fun at Transitions today. Jodi waltzes in while we're finishing lunch, and she's all heels and legs and silk blouse with a smile on top. For some reason, her presence today irritates the hell out of me.

"I hear, Robert," she fairly trills, "you've found a wonderful apartment." She laughs; her teeth sparkle and wink at Brett. The other clients are pulled away, and it is only Jodi and Brett and I here now.

"Such good things happening so quickly for you," she says. "You must be thrilled."

I bury my chin into my chest and won't look up at her, instead staring at my contracted hand.

"What's the matter?" she asks, and I ask myself the same question. The truth is I have become uneasy the last day or two as talk of apartment and independence has begun to bear fruit in the tangibles of furniture-hunting and an actual place to live.

"Nothing's the matter," I say.

She kneels down in front of me, leans forward, bends her head under mine, forces the gaze of her large eyes into mine.

"Cold feet, Robert?" she asks in that singing voice of hers. "It wouldn't be surprising," she says, "to be a little nervous now that your dreams are close to coming true."

My dreams? I am close to laughing. What can she know of my dreams, my fantasies? I shut my eyes against her, trying to think this through. Certainly I'm uneasy about the choices thrown at me, the new responsibilities I am threatened with. The novelty of folding laundry, of making lousy bologna sandwiches, is wearing off. Hey folks, I want to shout, the game's over. Now may I return to total dependence on staff?

But there's something else bugging me I can't quite nail down. Maybe it's a fear that, in the end, it is all just a game. Am I really making any choices? My life's still being directed and will be even in my own apartment that will swarm with caregivers most of the hours of each day. Who's kidding who? I know already Rehab and group home staff have their heads filled with plans for me, and they will meet with me and offer me a wonderful package and they will talk sweetly to me, like Brett did in the accessible apartment, and I will be led to think all this is what I want—yet goddamnit, they can't even get me a place with a bathtub.

"Who will be my roommate?" I ask Jodi.

"We've talked about Freddie," she says. "You know him from Transitions and Male Call. He can't afford his rent anymore and needs a place and a roommate to share expenses."

"Freddie's crazy," I say, though in truth I like him.

"We're all a little crazy," Brett says. "Anyway, he's just one option, and maybe not the best, since he's able to walk and doesn't need all those accessibility modifications. Ideally, we'd like to have another wheelchair guy in there."

"I thought I was going to walk."

"With assistance," Brett says. "Remember that's what we decided would be safe. Staff could walk you once a day."

"Bullshit," I say. "Fucking liar." I'm suddenly enraged and, I know, unintelligible. Brett's face instantly hardens, and he rises, looks at the area around me, looks at Jodi, who has gotten off her knees, whose large eyes retain their laughter, though mixed now with a speck of worry. Meanwhile Brett, I figure, is judging what damage I can do to the place or to Jodi or myself, if I get angry enough.

"Robert," Jodi says, like an affectionate, but stern, school marm, "you will apologize and explain yourself."

She is so ludicrous I can't help but laugh and feel my anger fade—fade, but not go away—fade into another part of me, stowed away for use later, for I feel I may need that anger fairly soon. Outwardly, I calm quickly, and force a smile onto Jodi who looks much too satisfied with herself. I swear I hear Brett sigh. I am not the only one who is nervous here.

At home, before dinner, I take stock of what I have, what my room holds and does not hold. It feels so bare, without carpet, with dirty white walls, with a twin bed and two small dressers, a grab bar near the bed, long metal kitchen table in the corner under the window where once I remember I used to sit and paint in my spare time, now covered with tablets, paper, a few books, magazines, a bowling trophy from when I used to bowl, and on the far wall, close to the wood sliding doors of the closet, is a Norman Rockwell poster of boys running from a swimming hole, and on the other wall a calendar of a few years past with a woman in hot pants holding a wrench, leaning across the hood of a red convertible, and the lone picture on my dresser of my son John, standing and smiling at the age of five-and-a-half in a yellow field and nothing, absolutely nothing behind him, but sky blue.

I have spent lifetimes within these barren walls.

And I would leave them now, for more lifetimes to come. I feel dimly ashamed, recalling Brett's comment about decorating my new apartment, that I have not done more in this room.

I am angry. I leave my room to roam the halls in my gleaming metal transport, looking for trouble, feeling mean, and others—staff and resident alike—seem to sense it since they all steer clear. "I want a tub; I want a fucking bathtub" is my mantra, focusing my anger, my frustrations. And poor Jimmy—do you remember Jimmy, the man of truly no brain from an earlier chapter of this tale? Poor Jimmy has no sense to stay out of my way. He comes next to me, stares at me with one of his puzzled looks.

"Roberto-o-o-o," he says. "It's ninety-nine degrees today in here, light and getting lighter. But no sun, you know?"

I yell, "Get away from me, you retarded piece of shit!" Or some such. I feel terrible instantly, picking on Jimmy, but I have no control left, and he is there.

"You make us all look like worse idiots than we are," I yell. "How come they don't put you away?"

Now Jennifer runs between us. Jimmy hasn't understood a word I've said, but he hears the rage, the insulting tone, and his face flushes hard in angry thought, trying to find the right response. His right leg shoots up and sneaks past Jennifer, kicking me in the foot.

"Goddamn," I roar, and charge through Jennifer, wheeling into her legs, knocking her off balance, out of my way, so I can reach Jimmy, and I throw wild punches at him, landing once or twice, till he, wild-eyed with fear, backs up quickly, howling like a wounded moose, though I know I have not connected with any authority. Jennifer is back now, red-faced, limping slightly, her eyes darkening in an anger which I cannot recall seeing in her before. She spins my chair like a top, sends me with one mighty shove backwards down my hall. She follows, and seems to calm, catches me and leans into my face: "In your room, Robert, for a while, till I can figure what to do about this. You know, I have to tell Brett and Jodi. Your whole program is based on your behavior."

With that, she steps out, closing the door, not with a slam, but not entirely silently either. I feel some small victory that I have overcome her professional detachment.

But I am not done. I breathe heavily, sag in my chair then determine they will not keep me closed in. These people have too much control. I need out.

But I am cautious. I open the door slowly and quietly, peek down the hall. I hear Jennifer speaking. Jimmy howls in the background, not in pain, but just being Jimmy. He probably has forgotten already what happened. I don't know where I want to go, just that I need to go. I wheel past Lorna's room and pause. I push the half-open door and peer in to see her propped up in bed, TV on at the foot of her bed, her eyes open as the changing lights of silent TV images flicker across her face. Her mouth holds a half grin, like she's complacent or half-crazy. The pain's been medicated away; she's reduced to a fog where neither I nor anyone else really exists to her.

I wheel to her bed and lean forward and whisper, "Lorna. Lorna. Lorna." She doesn't answer; she retains her silly grin. Her eyes don't follow the images on the TV. "Damn it," I say louder, more savagely. And as I stare at her face in the flickering lights, I imagine her eyes begin to focus, the goofy smile fades, intelligence returns, and she turns her head to me. Sitting straight up, she pulls the tubes from her arms and swings her legs over the side of the bed. Her legs are tanned brown, not the chalk white they had faded into. She rises and as she rises my heart leaps, my own legs stir with vitality, half-lifting me up. She stands above me, bare-breasted, leans into me, holds my face between two strong soft hands with long brown fingers, and she smiles before she kisses me, closes her mouth over mine, sucks my breath into her body, blows her breath into mine. I collapse backwards, my body filling each groove and corner of my chair, and then my broken head sighs upward, levitates below her lips, aside her breasts. I stretch my arms out to the sides of her, in victory and in ecstasy. God, I am weightless; I am rising up and up in currents of her acceptance.

I stand, unassisted, beside her. We are two whole people with a life before us, living, breathing each other.

Our light changes. The TV broadcasts a night scene, and our space is darkened. I glance over and see two Hollywood lovers in bed, pretending the act, creating fantasies. My body shivers as I lower myself back to the confines of my chair. Prone, in bed, amidst her tubes, Lorna's face still wears the half grin. I am nearly crying.

"What, what," I shout to her blank face, "could we have had?" But she lies there, so fogged, so stupid, so dead and dying, unseeing, unhearing. She is gradually wasting into nothing. We will be nothing, not even a pause in time.

"Damn," I roar and unlock my seat belt, push myself up from my chair, launch myself onto her bed. She barely groans, though her grin finally disappears as I land heavily and lock my arms around her to keep from sliding off the bed. Clumsily I arrange myself next to her and begin to claw, digging under her sheets, to find her legs, her hidden parts.

"How dare you be dying?" I whisper. "How dare you just lie here? Wake up, Lorna; they're killing you."

I don't pay any mind to tubes and catheters, so she groans and fixes an eye on me that seems genuinely scared and pained. I feel the warm soak of her urine as I dislodge her catheter, but still I push against her to kiss her, to grab some intimate part of her. Her body feels cold, as though she is nearly out of this world. Draping an arm across her chest, I pull her into me as close as possible and try to warm her. My spastic left leg involuntarily kicks her, and I am ashamed. We lie still then, together, her under the umbrella of my arm, me tunneling to be even closer to her body which is so cold on

top yet warm in her urine below. My chest moves in and out with her, and I glimpse her wild scared eyes as she peers at me, till there seems to come a flash of recognition, a calm in her look, an approval.

"Lorna," I whisper.

"Definitely," she replies.

We have found a moment to remember.

Then cold hands and harsh voices attack me from behind. Staff yell and pull on me, dump me unceremoniously on the floor. Jennifer stands over me, crying, then leans over Lorna, trying to help. Another staff runs out to phone a nurse.

Jennifer fusses over Lorna, gathers up her various tubes, then drops them and sits heavily onto the bed and sighs, tears wetting her cheeks. She looks down on me:

"Why Robert? Why?" She asks as though I have answers, and something about the question makes me laugh, which I am aware enough to know is inappropriate, but I have no control and can't stop even when I see Jennifer's eyes harden and meanness emerges where I have never seen it before.

I do stop laughing and hang my head in appropriate shame. Truly I feel the fool. I am smarter than what I have done, I say to myself, I am smarter than this . . .

I feel myself falling deep into a hole. I am afraid I will never return to the surface, never again suck down air from a bright blue sky, wave my arms over my head with a kind of joy. So many years I have been falling; since my accident I have been falling. Is there no bottom to this pit? Can I not one day finally be free of the rage that weighs around my neck, that anchors me, pulls me down, downward, continuously down?

A staff person comes from behind, bends, pushes his arms through mine, locks his hands across my chest and in a quick thrust lifts me to my waiting chair.

"God, you stink," the staff person says to me. He mutters under his breath about finding a new job.

I sit and smile, remembering my moment with Lorna. I know staff will report this. It will be recorded as so awful, so inappropriate that I will have to bear reproaches and counseling and stricter controls—though something in my soul screams the moment was worth what I will have to suffer. The moment was a ledge that temporarily halted my fall, more intense and authentic than our other encounters, united as we were in the puddles of her warm urine, a place more serene and intimate than I have ever been.

From the bed, Jennifer stares at me, though the hardness in her eyes has transformed into wondering, into sympathy. Or it may be pity, I suppose. She is condescending to the poor brain-injured man I am, but her look feels honest and open, and she is a human being I can rely upon. I know I need friends of any stripe and will not soon dismiss her from my side.

22

Retribution is swift and comes from all corners. There will be meetings, Jodi warns. What progress have I made or not made since Transitions, everyone wants to know. Is the state wasting its money on me?

At home, staff keep constant eye on me, and they have installed an alarm across Lorna's doorway. Only Jennifer treats me with the old kindness.

At Transitions, Brett frowns as he listens to me pound on the piano. He unfolds sheet music in front of me—"Ode to Joy"—and asks me to play anything other than Christmas music. I might not continue with them here, he says. "We haven't done our job." Otherwise, it is an uneventful day at Transitions. I do no walking, no household tasks. I spend most of the day just tagging along with Brett or killing time with other clients.

Then Jodi visits and tells me things are on hold for now: Transitions, apartment, etc. While the experts reevaluate.

I go to my old day program and Ellen comes. Even she, who has always remained distant enough from my personal problems to be nonjudgmental, comments on her disgust with what I have done. I am smarter than that, she reminds me.

We sit side by side at a long table, each before a computer. The sounds from her are like muffled machine gun fire as she blazes her words across the keyboard. Meanwhile I stare at my computer keys, at the plastic guard a therapist has rigged onto the board so I hit only one key at a time (and it protects the keys from my drool). I regret my gnarled hands and fingers that are so inflexible typing remains slow and difficult. Staring at my left hand, always half-closed unless I force it open, even after the operation, still lacking the stretch to reach from B to Q on the keyboard, I study its awkward contours, the veins spidering through the valleys between the bulging knuckles, the sparse black hairs on the backside, the callus that has grown on the side of my thumb, the ring finger which has grown thick, as though perpetually swollen, and has begun to twist outward doubling back on the little finger. I can no longer imagine having a healthy hand. I have grown used to what I have, and I'm surprised even to feel a certain fondness for my hand the way it is.

I am tired of writing this story, I tell Ellen. There will never be an ending.

Quick, write these feelings down, she exhorts.

I'm tired of trying to remember what has happened each day, of then trying to re-create what I think may have happened. I am writing nothing but lies and exaggerations, self-pitying whines, overanalysis. And I'm sure I've got it all remembered wrong; it's become all fiction. And to what purpose anymore? I take breaks from the computer, speak into my tape recorder since my speech is faster than my fingers. I break from that even, and sit with my hands folded across my lap, in front of the monitor with its white background and black letters that seem to shimmer, then dance as I watch them strive to break from the screen where I've nailed them, where I've had the nerve to believe I've given them significance by placing them there in the order I've chosen. They wink at me, and I swear I see them dance some more and leapfrog over each other or tumble down to other lines, making their own order and patterns, spilling out a nonsense that is beyond me, as though someone just pounded on the keys for a while or some crazy chimp was let loose on the keyboard. The more I stare the less able I am to make sense of what is written. There is no permanence to what is there. I have not caught memories in a bottle. I have nothing on screen or paper but the ravings of a man who can't remember, who can't fix things long enough in his head to get his impressions in any shape that might be recognizable as reality.

I'm tired, tired of the attempt. Yet I can't live, I can't function without pattern or routine. If you change my room, it will take me weeks to comfortably find my way to the bathroom by myself. I am head-injured. I must find the structure and order of all things or I don't function.

Feeling a warmth on my shoulder, I shake my head and break from my thoughts. "Relax," Ellen whispers as she leans over me. "Do you need to lie down?"

I need a rest from so much thought, a vacation from the stress. Maybe Transitions and prospects of independence have brought a lot more stress, she says, than people have realized.

"Have you talked with your family lately?" she asks. "How's your son?"

"He's fine," I say curtly and dismissively, then add quickly, "How're your children?"

"They come and go," she says. "They live out of town, you know. Never enough time for much visiting."

Funny, I think. I have so much time.

"Part of what you did with Lorna is due to your injury," Doctor Larry says in our special session, hurriedly arranged by Transitions staff. "Your injury has robbed you of sound judgment and impulse control. But we thought you were more capable than this. You have seriously jeopardized your chances of living more independently in the community."

I give no reply. Indeed, I have been quiet throughout our meeting, though I know my silence only hurts my cause. I should be expressing appropriate remorse, assuring them I have learned, promising I will do better.

But I feel stubborn today.

"Why do you think you did it?" Doctor Larry asks for the third or fourth time.

I breathe quietly through his frustrated sighs, his halting exhortations, his warnings that my future lies in the balance here. Finally, I decide to give him a bone:

"I want a bathtub when I move," I say.

"That's it?" he says, and looks at me with astonishment. "Because of that, you had your rage? That's why you attacked Lorna?"

"I didn't attack Lorna. What I did was dangerous, and I'm sorry. Let's move on to other issues. Like my bathtub."

Poor Doctor Larry shakes his head.

"What will we do, Robert, with you?"

"Give me my tub," I mumble, refusing appropriateness.

Grinding on, Doctor Larry decides he will readminister psych tests to me, compare how I am with how I was when I first started Transitions. My immediate future promises meetings and tests to measure and chart my progress, he says.

"You seem unwilling to cooperate today," he says. "Maybe we'll try again in a couple days. But I don't want you to forget what we're working towards here."

I don't have a clue what he's talking about, and he's about to dismiss me when I feel a desperation set in. Yeah, I like sitting here quiet. Sometimes silence is the only control I have over an event. But now when he's threatening to leave me, I must speak, hold him here a little longer.

"I didn't mean to hurt her," I say. "Though I knew I could hurt her. It's just that . . ." and here I pause, fearing I will not be able to explain what they all see so clearly as an inappropriate event. "I didn't think it through. I don't remember what I was thinking when I went into her room. But I don't feel sorry now. I don't think Lorna is sorry for what I did."

"Then we can't trust you," Doctor Larry says.

"I won't do it again," I tell him. "I got what I wanted."

"And what was that?"

"I don't know," I honestly say.

Doctor Larry frowns, then leans forward into my face. "What is it you want?" he asks.

"I don't know," I repeat, then remember what Ellen had told me. "I want a rest."

The good doctor leans back in his swivel chair, puts one hand behind his head, adjusts his tie with the other.

"You've been working hard." He nods his head.

23

I am leaving western Montana. At least for a week or two. An enforced vacation while the experts confer about my fate.

We—Jennifer and I—drive from Missoula to Whitefish, where I will meet my dad and the Amtrak train that will take us home to Wolf Brook. At Ellen's insistence, I carry my trusty tape recorder. She promises to help transcribe when I get back.

The drive is two hours through the Mission Mountains and pine forests, broad valleys and pastureland, and the Flathead Indian Reservation. Not quite halfway there we descend into St. Ignatius, into the valley, headed to the town over which the black jagged white-capped Mission Mountains loom. A born flatlander, I am unsettled by the stark drama of the landscape and the dreams such drama can inspire. Here, I fear, people can lose sight of what life means. They begin to doubt why our routines mean so much, why a rancher may rise at dawn, why we all drag ourselves each morning to jobs, why we remain by the side of the people we've chosen.

Jennifer is mostly quiet as she drives us through St. Ignatius. From grassy hillsides, bison shake their unruly heads, and we speed past Ninepipe, where mountains mingle in the reflections of valley wetlands, where trees sprout from unlikely islands, where men dream in canoes of big fish, under the tall shadows of the Missions. Our car rides a high plateau then through valleys and towns before dipping and curving again with the road till we get our first glimpse of the long slender Flathead Lake and the tourist towns dotting its coast.

“There,” Jennifer shouts and points a finger past my nose, breaking our quiet. “I saw the Flathead Lake monster.”

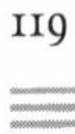

Instinctively, gullibly, I cast my eyes the way of her finger and, of course, see nothing but the wavy dark green of the water surface.

“Did you see him?” Jennifer says. “A long scaly serpent.” She laughs, the first laugh of our road trip.

I want to be angry at her for fooling the head-injured guy, but her laughter is contagious.

“Yeah,” I snort, and break up convulsively. “He looks like Doctor Larry.”

She laughs again. We stop for drinks and so I can go to the bathroom.

I don’t recall ever taking the train before, though over the phone Mom said I did once in my real life before “The Fall,” when I was in college. She said my dad doesn’t trust his eyesight or stamina enough to make the trip by car anymore.

Jennifer and I make Whitefish in barely enough time as she curses road construction and slow drivers. We’re running late, she says, as we get out of the car and go down Whitefish’s wooden walkways to the restaurant where we’re to meet Dad. Tourists stride past us in painted cowboy boots as Jennifer wheels me past storefront windows featuring silver buckles and turquoise necklaces. Despite our rush, she can’t help but pause with each passerby, searching for celebrity faces. Red, green, and blue pamphlets seem to dangle everywhere promising nearly year-round soft powder in the mountains for passionate skiers. “There’s Julia Roberts across the street,” Jennifer squeals in my ear. “She has a home around here, you know.”

“Yeah, her and the Flathead monster,” I say, then I spot Dad through a window, sitting in the restaurant, uncomfortably alone, in old jeans, cowboy shirt with snaps instead of buttons: an east-slope Montanan out of place, a cigarette dangling from the corner of his mouth. I remember him chewing tobacco, smoking the occasional cigar, but I don’t remember cigarettes. When we enter, he rises, snuffs out the cigarette in an ashtray. Gracefully—I remember noting—gracefully he pulls a chair out for Jennifer and, with his foot, pushes another one out of the way so my wheelchair can fit.

“Do you want coffee?” he asks Jennifer.

“We’re running a little late,” she says. “I’m sorry.”

"Yeah, we should probably get to the train station," Dad says.

"When did you start on cigarettes?" I say and try to smile.

"Just one now and then," he says with a grimace. "I didn't want you to see." He blows out smoke he had kept in a hidden pocket of his cheeks.

Once we are settled on board the train—Dad in his seat, me braked in an open space next to him—he tries to shoot the bull with me, but we had seen each other not so long ago and not much news has accumulated. He drifts into an old man's tired sleep, which is fine with me. I am content. A quiet trip home along the High Line down from the mountains to the plains.

I pull out the tape recorder and record what I see on the way home, like the names on the railway and highway signs, announcing stations or places of interest:

Whitefish. West Glacier. Blackfeet Reservation.

After the Divide, the land flattens out. Mountains are distant and alien. Billboards announce dinosaur country where low hills are rocky with sparse weeds, where I find it hard to imagine any life as big as the dinosaur bones they pull out of here.

Cut Bank. Joplin. Inverness. Kremlin. Rocky Boy Reservation.

Dry stony beds remember seasonal streams. Other than cottonwoods, which signal muddy waters, vegetation seems reduced to brown weeds and pale green sage which always looks ready to dry up at any moment, to break loose, to become tumbleweed. I want to say there is a lack of drama on the plains, but drama is here, just more under the surface than in the mountains. You can keep your breath here and contemplate the small things.

Havre. Chinook. Zurich. Fort Belknap Reservation.

Private dumps in the shallow hollows: rusted orange appliances, old trucks. This is ancient dying country, windswept, a few clapboard houses, then light blue mobile homes with fragile post fences arrayed around them, 4-by-4 trucks, and faded signs that introduce towns too small to be train stops.

Harlem. Malta. Vandalia. Glasgow. Fort Peck Reservation.

In Malta, a bank clock says 102 degrees. The sun shining in late July on the High Line is merciless, and I remember walking a lane on the ranch and feeling all there is to my world is blinding sun and dust. Hammerin Hank's Autobody advertises on the side of a cement block garage and McDonald's golden arches prove the High Line is not above all civilization. Men stroll in old boots and new stiff jeans. A sign for a one-story motel blinks, stuck on "Vacancy."

Out of Malta I know I am getting close to home. The images resonate with more familiarity, rolling past my window like a mist out from the past. Pastures are dotted with brown rolls of hay and occasional gray barns, faded green John Deeres, rows of telephone pole sentries, shadowless cattle that look thin in the wide landscape. Just before the Fort Peck Reservation, I see, at one corner of a fenced pasture, two horses standing in the wind, right next to each other, each facing opposite directions so they are head to butt and butt to head. I want to wake Dad, to ask him why horses stand like that. I remember my brother being thrown from a horse, rounding up cattle—or were we just playing? The hard dried ground with prickly weeds and a yelp of pain. A steer kicked up his heels to escape the activity. The horse bolted home, and I looked down to my brother's arm all crooked and bent the wrong way. I don't remember anything more, but I must have gotten him home.

Wolf Brook.

It lies just inside the reservation, bordering the Missouri, where, history books say, flatboats once delivered goods and trappers. Suddenly, I feel short of breath. I don't ever remember feeling comfortable here, though I try to focus long enough to search my long-term memory for moments of peace, and I know there are some. The ranch. My father. My brother and sister. And school friends and dances and the dirt-bike rides along the hills and shallow gullies. I had a life here, and I don't know why I left or why I feel now so out of place, so threatened, especially when I first see the railway sign, "Wolf Brook," and on the concrete platform, Mom and my brother, Cyrus. The train station is not at all familiar to me, though this town is too small for me to ever have missed the station. I must wake my dad, tell him we are here. Funny that I have this responsibility for him now.

But I don't want to get out; I don't want the train to stop. I want to continue east. I've never been east, have I? My mom has family in North Dakota, and maybe I was there when I was a kid, but that's not east enough. I'm desperate to keep traveling, almost ready to shout, leave me be, even as a conductor appears from behind to wheel me off the train. You don't understand, I try to say; I can't stop here in Wolf Brook. I must keep traveling east—or go back to Missoula. I must.

Strangers don't understand my words. Dad takes over for the conductor and wheels me to my family. Mom stands with one hand shading her eyes, then glances at her wristwatch, maintains her worried look even though the train has safely arrived. She wears a blue dress and a scarf over her hair and low-cut tennis shoes, and she finally breaks from her stance to come to me, to bend down and hug me, her smell the smell of faded lilacs at the end of spring. Cyrus approaches and spits out a long brown string of tobacco juice, splashing my wheels and his own dusty boots. He smiles his goofy yellow-toothed smile, as though to tell me I should have stayed home on the ranch a long time ago. I didn't have to go to college, to climb mountains.

24

Off the pavement, the roads are brown and dusty and rocky. Little stones pit the windshield with regularity. I remember the barbwired land, the infrequent dips and rises, the occasional lonely tree which shades a steer or two, the tall grass flowing in the ever-present wind. These scenes are locked in my long-term memory. In winter, the wind will stripe the road with heavy snow drifts and bare dirt. A few cattle will be found broken down on the plain, maybe near a frozen-over creek, dead, eyes and mouth frozen open, nostrils flared, as if they were caught in angry surprise, the pain still a grimace on their long faces.

In summer the roads are dust, and dust kicks up around and behind us as Cyrus drives his truck fast down our ranch roads: Mom and Dad squeezed in the small rear area behind the seats, me and Cyrus like two teenagers again in the front seats, windows down, Mom complaining about the dust and the wind in her hair, and Dad alternating between laughs and moans, grousing about the seasonal lack of water and his arthritic knees. There, I try to say above the rush of wind, the sputtering of the truck, in that barrow pit, Cyrus and I . . . but no one can understand me, and I can't remember what I was saying after all. But there are memories on this land. I feel them, though they don't drop easily unscrambled from my brain.

"Please put up the window, Cyrus," Mom shouts, and Cyrus complies. She doesn't ask the same of me. "I remember when you and Cyrus and Emmy were just little," she yells to us in the front seat.

"You remember, Robbie? Back in real life. Over there, under the cottonwoods, by the creek, you and Cyrus nearly hanged your little sister. Don't know what you were thinking, tying her up like that."

Cyrus laughs. I don't remember any such incident, though the cottonwoods look familiar. As I'm jostled by a pothole in the road I begin to remember the creek that runs by there, the cutbank under the tree roots where once I netted a few tadpoles. Cyrus looks over at me and smiles in embarrassment. I don't ever recall him as talkative, and since my accident, I feel he is uncomfortable around me, that he is always searching for words, and never quite finds them. Occasionally, he reminisces about when we were kids, though I don't remember specifics. He generally avoids the present.

"Hey Rob," he says now, "You want to have a drink with me at Stockman's? Maybe see some of the old fellows? Lots of folks still ask about you, especially if they don't see you around the holidays."

"Sure." I nod.

"Good," Cyrus says. But I get the feeling we won't ever do it. I'd like to ask him about his family—the wife and kids—but I can't remember names.

The white house where I grew up still perches on a slight rise with a willow and a birch on each side, a barn and garage straddling the driveway, wood and metal corrals circling the area. Mom talks about their plans of moving into town, letting Cyrus and his family move from down the lane into this, the big house. "Your dad can't help Cyrus much anymore anyways," she says, and Dad clears his throat and Cyrus says, "Dad still works like when he was young, just up a little later and down a little sooner."

"Goddamn cows," Dad says. "I wouldn't miss them if I was in town." He says it after we've stopped, after Cyrus is out of the truck and helping Dad get out from the back area, and Dad is looking around the place, and I think I know his look. I imagine his routine of giving everything the quick once-over upon his return. He will not go quickly into the house. First he'll walk through the barn, check the amount of feed stored, walk a little ways around the fences near the house, stop at the watering hole, run a hand through his hair, and then he'll come in. His routine.

There is a place in the far corners of our property which is left unfenced, where the plain and the sky meet in dignity, where sagebrush is dense, where Cyrus and Dad and I used to hunt pronghorn with our .22 rifles and snuff in our cheeks. I remember how a pronghorn leaps on being approached, dashes with worried speed, horns seeming to curl back in the wind as it jumps for escape, and the shot barking, the sound following the bullet into hide and flesh, and if you get there quick enough, you see the smoke rise from the hole in the body, you smell the blood. This cruel life, I remember a man once argue, in which hunters seek out the biggest, the most impressive of the species to kill, unlike the natural selection of your animal predators who cull the weakest, the sickest, the most disabled of the herd. Civilized Man, of course, is no longer a natural predator, though we are left with this cruel life of the rancher where cattle are raised for nothing else than quick weaning, early death, unnatural slaughter, where a horse with a broken leg is put down. No questions, no pity. I love the wind along the plain in what would otherwise be the unbearable heat of an Eastern Montana summer, the cracks and furrows of old rancher faces, that have endured the weather, the bent bowlegs of cowboys, the whinnies of horses being broken, this cruel harsh place where it is too damned hard to be feeble.

On the porch stands John, face tanned and still adolescently plump, the shadow of a mustache above his lip, leaning on a post, waiting as Cyrus arranges my wheelchair near the car door, then helps me take the long step down from his truck. The chair nearly scoots away when I plop down. Cyrus has forgotten the brake. But I settle safely, and my sister Emmy appears alongside John, and behind her are younger kids, hers and Cyrus's, gathered for me, as if this is some grand family reunion. The paint on the porch is flaking, the floor seems to sag, and I wonder if it will hold the weight of all these people and my chair too. The ramp to the side built so many years ago by Dad and Cyrus is weathered and splintering. I laugh with a thought of the group home, where things are kept clean and up-to-date and safe, not like here, this real world home. I would like to stay out here, in the air. In fact, I would love to go with Dad on his quick tour and check of the place, but Emmy comes down and grabs my chair by the back and starts to wheel me up the ramp to the waiting horde of kids whose names I can never recall.

"Nice to see you, Robert," John says. "Dad," he corrects himself.

He offers a hand, which I take, and I pull him down so we hug. He stays with me a long moment and doesn't try to pull away.

"Come on, kids," Emmy wails to my nephews and nieces. "Greet your uncle properly."

But they recoil at my wheelchair, my drooling mouth, my strangled efforts at speech. I reach out to shake hands, to hug small bodies, but they scatter to the corners or escape off the porch edges.

"You know how kids are, Rob," Emmy sighs. "But you wait and see what Mom and I have planned for you."

"We've all been just so thrilled," Mom says, "with you in that Transitions program where you can get better." She looks at me carefully, on the lookout for obvious improvements. I see her brow furrow, her hand fly to her face. She exchanges looks with Emmy.

"We're having a party for you," Emmy says in a voice that almost seems a groan.

That evening there is a party, lots of food and drink, with most of my family turned out and a few neighbors and some people from town. They have me set at a table where Mom can watch me, watch what I eat, and ensure that I refuse the alcohol offered me. Occasionally Emmy takes her place beside me, helping me with my plate. Guys I don't remember shake my hand, women come and speak with Emmy or Mom, smile at me and speak a few pleasant words. Once I grab for the grape juice Mom had poured for me, but the lid on the plastic cup is not on tight and the juice spills over me, over Emmy's dress, dribbles down the white tablecloth, onto the carpet. Emmy wheels me to my room to help me clean up while Mom excuses herself to the bathroom.

"I'm tired. I want to go to bed now," I say to Emmy, who's helping get my shirt off. I have to sit up straight, swallow my spit, and repeat myself before she understands.

"The evening's young," she says. "All these people have come to see you."

"The show's over." I give her a slight push away when she starts to undo my pants. "I can dress and undress myself."

"I'm sorry, Rob. We thought things were getting easier for you. People came to visit, not to stare."

I am about to scream at her, but something in the way she bends, in the way she holds my stained shirt in her hands, reminds me of earlier days when she was my kid sister and I would tease her and I could choose to either make her cry or squeal with laughter. A scene flashes of her laughing once when I threw a wrinkled shirt at her, asking her to iron it.

"Kelsey was supposed to come," she says. "But it's getting kind of late now."

"Who's Kelsey?" I say.

"Why, John's mother. You remember her."

"Help me get dressed," I say, though I feel I will be making a large mistake to go back out there.

I am right. Mom has been drinking and she gushes at the sight of me reemerging from my room. She gives a wink at Emmy and takes my chair and bumps me through family to the old upright piano, sitting black and dusty along the dining room wall. Except now, it has been recently tuned, Mom tells me.

"I'm sure everybody remembers how well you played. You used to be so wonderful. They tell us you still play at the day program."

The smell of alcohol on her breath disorients me. She rarely touches a drop, and I can't remember her ever drunk, but here she is now, shoving me into the piano, leaning heavily onto my chair so she doesn't stumble herself, whispering some nonsense at me, then clapping her hands for the attention of her company.

"Robbie was a great piano player in his real life," she announces as people quiet down. "I remember seeing his recital in Missoula. He wore a tux. I was so proud. It was Beethoven, wasn't it, Robbie?" I scan the faces desperately for Dad, thinking he might rescue me, but I can't find him and think he's probably outside, comfortable, checking his cattle, his fences. Cyrus is half-asleep in an easy chair with a beer in his hand. John looks away from a girl he's with to watch me. He seems unsure of what to do.

"Robbie, play a song for the people," Mom says.

"You're drunk," I tell her, but no one understands me. The people seem to gather closer. Their faces are uncomfortable. I remember being an oddity among them, the ranch kid playing classical music, putting on airs.

Emmy kneels beside me, grabs my hand, and whispers, "Just a little something for Mom. You don't mind. Then she'll let you go." Her voice grows louder then, so others can hear: "One of your Christmas carols, Rob. We'll have Christmas in July."

Angrily I turn from her and bang on the piano keys. I stretch the fingers of my left hand out as far as I can, trying to reach eight keys of the octave. I don't know what I play: perhaps it is "O Holy Night," or "The First Noel," or "Ode to Joy." I feel the music flow from my fingers. I feel them dance along the keyboard lightly, correctly stroking the appropriate keys, crescendos coming in place, then softer melodies floating from my hands across the room. I'm doing well, better than I can ever remember. I am amazed, then entranced, safe, away from the crowd, inside the music, inside my private meditation, where these people cannot enter. And now I can stretch from middle C to high C, as I stroke the keys effortlessly, even lovingly. Oh, this sound that breaks like waves around me, flushing deep into the corners of my mind and soul, and I am out on the flat land again under the big azure sky and bleached cumulus clouds lifting me tenderly to a destination beyond this

. . . till there's a poke into my shoulder that wakens me from this trance, that returns me to my parents' ranch house dining room.

Dad tells me, "Enough," and my hands stop then fall heavily, discordantly, upon the keys, as I look up into the withered face of my father. I peek around me. Little kids have their hands over their ears. Most of the crowd has retreated into other rooms or spilled into the night outside. Emmy is crying, kneeling beside me. Mom has disappeared.

I wheel to my room, and this time Emmy doesn't follow to convince me to return. I slam the door behind me as best I can, cursing, wishing I could fling myself from my chair to the bed in one fast fluid motion. I hear voices of family and guests filter through the door. I feel so frustrated I pound my good hand on my wheelchair arm, hurting my hand and nearly spilling me sideways and out. But the pain feels good, somehow, and I feel good, to be alone, in my childhood room, to have no caregivers around, where I can let down my guard and cry.

It is not too long before Emmy comes in and helps me undress, to get ready for bed.

25

The big double door entrance to the back of the barn is up a small rise, large enough to admit tractors and trucks. Cyrus and John struggle to push me up and in. Pretty soon this space will be filled with bales of straw, but now the floor is clear, and instinctively I look to the rafter where still there is the basketball backboard Dad nailed up when Cyrus and I were kids. John picks up and dribbles, clumsily, an old slippery basketball that has lost its bounce. He shoots from the corner, and misses rim, backboard, everything. He grins sheepishly at me and his uncle.

"I haven't shot a basketball in years," Cyrus says, and he looks funny in his cowboy boots and jeans, bending over to retrieve the ball. While bent over, he spits a stream of tobacco juice. He balances the ball awkwardly in one hand, takes careful aim and shoots. The ball bounds noisily off the rim, almost into my face. John grabs it and hands it to me.

"I don't play," I say and let the ball roll off my lap.

"You used to," Cyrus says, and I remember long one-on-one sessions after dark in the dim lights of the barn, playing with Cyrus, trying to beat him, but he was bigger and stronger, and it seems I landed often in the straw bales lining the sides of the court, bounced none too gingerly there by Cyrus, who refused to acknowledge his fouls.

"You used to be a decent shot," Cyrus says and hands me the ball again.

“Fine,” I say, and throw the ball up, in the general direction of the hoop. I have lots of strength but little control with my left hand and arm. The ball sails over rim and backboard, into a dark corner of the barn where shovels and rakes are stored.

“Goddamnit,” Cyrus says. “You should play that wheelchair basketball.”

“Shut up, Cyrus.” I glare at him; he has no sense of my disability.

“Sure thing,” Cyrus says and shakes his head, then stares at me. “I just came to give John a hand pushing you up here. I’ll go down to the house awhile.”

Cyrus leaves. I sit off to the side, while John shoots baskets, now swishing them with some consistency. He stops for a moment to smile at me, a small line of sweat broken just under his hairline.

“Mom’s coming today,” he says then resumes his basketball.

My son John’s mom.

I hate to admit how it bothers me that I can’t remember her, not a whit, nothing. She’s from another time, another place. There are some things, the doctors confirm, from right before the accident I have no memory of: for instance, the fall itself (though I have created images, filled in the gaps). But Kelsey (that’s her name, I’m told) was enough before the fall that I should remember her, at least as well as other persons and places of that time, and of course I knew Kelsey better than most. I think I even remember bits of her family, dark-skinned and large-boned (she’s a quarter-Assiniboine, John says). I hold an image of a dark house, with low voices from the dark, and a rattling of beads, marking doorways, instead of doors, and a frayed couch with doilies on the back. But no image of Kelsey, almost as though I am in those scenes by myself.

There comes a regularity in John’s dribbling and shooting, in the thumping of the ball on wooden floor and backboard, and I fall half-asleep, half-dreaming of this ranch, of a time when I come in from chores looking for breakfast and Mom has pancakes on the griddle and Cyrus and Dad come in after me. We have worked hard and we are hungry. Emmy enters from the living room, sleepy-eyed, hair in pigtails, and we all sit to what feels now like an eternal meal spread before my mind, a snapshot that captures some idyllic moment.

One evening, Mom shouts up the stairs to me, “You’re going to be late for the dance. Cyrus is waiting in the truck for you.”

“I think going to the university is the best thing for a boy like you,” Dad said one day. “Wolf Brook ain’t exactly a place you want to be stuck in. You should at least have options.”

“He was the educated one, the smart one,” Dad said later to friends, emphasizing the past tense, speaking as if I wasn’t there, as though a wheelchair makes you invisible. “Cyrus was the athlete.”

Mom recalls when Dad let her stay in Missoula after my accident for a couple months to be with me while Emmy took care of things at home and neighbors raised a fund to help pay for things like Mom’s stay in Missoula. I was like a baby, she says; she had to teach me how to talk and dress and go to the bathroom all over again. I suppose the hospital staff helped a bit, she says, but they certainly weren’t anywhere around after she took me home. Emmy helped some, and Cyrus and Dad, but mostly, she says, it was her, raising her son a second time, a second chance to mold me the right way. And then we found out Kelsey had my child on the way. I never doubted it, my mom says, never questioned it, like your dad who said Kelsey was just after our money, like we had any money to be after. Well, there’s our land, your dad says, our operation. You mean, a lot of backache and miserable hours, she says she told him. I was thrilled, she says, to have a grandchild, someone to take your place, now that you were hurt. A gift, that’s what John has been, a gift from God, who works in His mysterious ways. I’ve given thanks every day for John. Do you remember when you first saw him, and I laid him in your lap, and you smiled like you were king of the hill? God, Robbie, I taught you everything, talked to you about everything, reminded you of every important thing of your real life.

As I sit in the barn, John shooting baskets, the sound of a car spinning into the gravel driveway wakes me from my thoughts. I hear a car door slam, a strange woman’s voice, then my mom’s voice. I turn and wheel towards the wide barn door where sunlight streams in.

“Long time no see,” a woman says, hand shaded over her eyes as she stands on the rise in the sun looking into the barn. I am struck by her high cheekboned beauty, her dark hair and complexion. She is thin and wears a jean skirt, a white blouse, sandals. “Can I come in?”

The basketball bounces then rolls into a wall. John is at my side, not saying a word.

"Sure, why not?" I say, but instantly see she doesn't understand so I gesture for her to come. John almost runs to the woman, but holds himself back. He smiles at her and says, "Hi, Mom."

This is Kelsey. I stare at her face, study her gait, but no memory of her is resurrected.

"I'm sorry," she says, "for waiting so long to visit."

"Have you visited before?" I ask. John asks me to repeat, then he interprets for her.

"I saw you after your accident," she says. "I went to Missoula once while you were in the hospital. I don't suppose you'd remember that. I saw you a couple times after you came back to Wolf Brook, and I brought John for you to see."

"Damn," I mutter, "I don't remember any of it."

"Well, then, they took you back to Missoula, to live in the group home. I meant to visit, but you know, there was the kid, and work, and stuff. Not that easy sometimes getting away. I've seen you occasionally when you're home. Though I never said anything. John keeps me informed how you are."

"How are you, Kelsey?" I draw out her name with emphasis, trying to lock it into my brain. Close up, she looks older; furrows have formed down from the sides of her nose to the corners of her mouth. There is gray sprinkled in her hair, and her eyes are too sad to watch for long.

"Oh me, I'm fine," she says. "Thanks for asking. It hasn't been a picnic, you know," she laughs nervously as she says it. "I was married to Henry Bumter. Do you remember him? I assume John tells you things. We split in the winter. John and I are still getting used to it. Living alone again."

"That's too bad," I say.

"I'm okay," she says. "I worry about John. Henry was no prince, but he was the only father . . . well, you know what I mean." She looks at the ground, then up, and shakes her hair behind her, regains composure. "Well, you look good," she says, though she avoids looking straight at me. "From what John says, you seem fixed up pretty well at the group home." She sits on a hay bale, crossing her legs, then rambles about people she says we knew, what's happening with them, who has kids, who's divorced, who should be. It's all another world to me, but I try to listen, try not to fade out into my own fantasies.

“Why did you come?” I ask.

“After all these years, I felt I should. And John wanted it. He says you’re getting better in that Transitions program.”

“You don’t have to be sorry for not visiting more often,” I tell her, and I feel awkward about the whole picture of her and me having ever been together. We are a basic mismatch, a mistake, and maybe this is why she doesn’t fit in my memories.

Somewhere from my mind’s recesses, images are launched, of other women. I don’t recall great successes with the sex opposite, but I remember from my college days some conquests and some failures, and one or two nights of talking when real connections were felt. Trickling into my brain from way back is a girl I knew who studied music, and we spent a night together speaking of classical versus rock, I think. Bits and pieces of conversation can emerge like this to haunt me, enough to remind me of what I used to be.

I think that girl and I used to talk about music and philosophy a lot. For us, these were things that mattered. Lunches on the campus lawn. Old Main clock broken and locked into an eternal ten minutes to. The whitewashed concrete M on the mountain watched over us. One night we walked up the zigzag trail to the M with nothing but stars and a quarter moon to light us and up there we said we would make love and sure enough we wrestled around a little. I remember a button on her blouse that would not come undone. I was nearly frantic at its resistance, till finally she laughed gently and pushed my clumsy hand away. It broke the lustful mood, but we lay next to each other for a good long time, and since neither of us knew the constellations, we made up our own and took each other’s hand to trace the connections we made between the stars.

Her name was Tricia, it comes to me now, though I’m never confident of the accuracy of the memories. I can’t lock onto her face at will, but it comes in intermittent waves, like so many things of the past. Where is she now, I wonder. Where are the folks I knew back in college? Odd only the Wolf Brook people retain any presence for me from my past.

Kelsey is from the High Line. When I struggle with the time frame, I figure she must come soon after college, maybe right when I returned. My mom says I had plans for graduate school but came back to Wolf Brook to work on the ranch for a while.

"Robert, Robert, where are you?" It's Kelsey shaking my arm, the first time, I think, she's touched me since her visit began.

"He loses concentration like that," John explains. "It's hard for him to stay focused."

"Well Robert, how about I buy us lunch in town," Kelsey says, and I admire her suddenly for trying to make the best of this. "John says he can help you into the car and he knows how to fold up your wheelchair so it'll fit in the trunk."

"Why not?" I say.

Lunch is a production with me, finding a place everybody likes that has access for my chair and room for me to fit alongside a table. And nothing too close to others I might offend with my eating habits. I'm long used to it, of course, but I'm always with staff or my parents, not with someone like Kelsey who is new to the whole thing. She grimaces and bears up like a good trooper, and I have sense enough to avoid messy items like soup or fried chicken. I order a hamburger, and John and Kelsey do the same. Safety somehow with the repetition.

She's a wealth of information about everyone we see, about every place we pass. Though I want to scream my indifference to the current Wolf Brook, I am finally impressed by the sheer volume of trivia of the place that she possesses and shares so easily.

Our food comes and she quiets for a moment, reflects as she bites and chews, then resumes, this time about John:

"He starts high school when summer's over," she says. John sits back, sizing us up, never having seen the two of us together before.

"What are you thinking, John?" I ask.

"Nothing," he says, but continues, "just about your Transitions program. Wondering how it's going."

"Great," I say and sit up straight, swallow, and speak slowly and as clearly as I can. "They say I'm talking better, and I'm able to walk with a walker. And my hand. Look at my hand." I place my left hand on the table and push down. The fingers spread; the palm almost lies flat on the table. When I look up at John's and Kelsey's faces, I see they're not impressed.

"That's great, Robert," Kelsey smiles sweetly and touches my arm and lets me study her face. Desperately I struggle to develop an image, to find a memory of her from my past. The intensity of the look on my face must scare her because she leans away from me.

"When did we meet?" I ask. John still helps to interpret.

"We went to grade school together," Kelsey fairly shrieks. "I was a year younger. You don't remember any of that?"

If I try hard, I can summon a few names and faces from back then. Kelsey has no place in any of them. I worry how I could have so completely misplaced her.

"When did we start going out?"

"During your last year of college," she says. "Over Christmas break. Like suddenly after all the years, we discovered each other. Then we went out again after you graduated and came back to Wolf Brook." She continues with stories that amaze me, akin to my own flights of imagination I can't trust to be true, but at the best of times, I call my memories. We fell into each other at the town Christmas festival, she says. We threw snowballs at each other, before we even recognized each other, and afterward ended up together, alone, probably drunk, driving the top of an icy levee in her brother's jeep (and here she sneaks a look at John, a don't-do-crazy-like-I-did look, and she winks at me). The riskiness of the stunt pulled us closer together than we might have ordinarily gotten. But then again, she says she had watched me from afar for a while, followed my college progress, had her hopes set on me, so to speak, for some time before that wild ride. I have recurrent dreams that have evolved into visions of long tunnels winding white through the dark, traveling by vehicle or on foot, perched on a high central line, and no end in sight. Do my dreams hold fragments of memories lost?

"That Christmas you were like a lost puppy. I suspected someone at college had broken your heart."

"I suppose so," I say. I look into her large brown eyes where images like a newsreel of my past seem to flicker, and what is it I think I see? Her dark hair swimming in the wind behind her, trailing out over the back end of an open jeep, in the dead dark white of winter. That was her; that was Kelsey. I'm foolishly elated at the recall, smile much too grandly and grab for her hand with too little tact, though I capture a moment of her devout attention. Our eyes lock, and maybe I remember the lonesome thrill of being touched, of being held by a woman who loves you. I can't say what I remember now, what are details and facts, but I feel a little of the original moments with her, as though a part of me other than intellect remembers her. I know without knowing how she was unlike the women of my college days: a High Line girl, born and bred, and would remain one no matter where she roamed, and I was, at all times then, aiming beyond the High Line. But she was there, in the icy air, attractive and willing.

"We dated a couple months after you came home from college," Kelsey says. "You said you loved me—the night before you left to go back to Missoula for your rock climbing trip."

She was there that summer of my fall. I can't remember my aspirations then, what I was planning, what I felt. Mom says I talked of graduate school in the east; Cyrus says I wanted a temporary job on a local ranch.

"I'm sorry," I tell Kelsey, though I'm not sure for what.

"You were handsome," she says. "And smart. I felt lucky to be with you, even to have your child, but I guess God didn't think I was supposed to be too lucky. You had your accident."

"God's gift," I mumble and am not understood.

John, initially fascinated by our talk, fidgets and seems to grow uncomfortable. He wants to change the subject.

"Mom's talking of going back to school. To the community college in Dawson."

"Well, now that Henry and I are split," she says and smiles. "I don't envision myself a store clerk all my life."

Suddenly I don't know where I am, like that TV show where the guy leaps into different people's bodies across time, and he has to spend a few hours just orienting himself to where and when and who he is. I look around the restaurant, then out the sunny windows that look out on a broad avenue with cars and trucks slipping by in a continuous line like one colorful disjointed snake. For a moment, I don't recognize John's and Kelsey's faces. They don't fit anywhere in my head, and what they're talking about becomes completely foreign: her ex-husband and trying to find work and John's high school next year. All that is ordinary for them is too difficult for me to follow. Yet I panic because I sense there's something essential here I should grasp. These people—my son, for Christ's sake—what's the relation now? Even as he sits inches away, we are as distant as the stars from the earth. He and she continue, talking to each other, as though I am not here, of a world of rent and car payments and band practice. They touch each other's arms, laugh comfortably with the intimacy of family, with intimacy that must come from sharing these small things. I am intensely sad as I focus on Kelsey's face, before escaping into a daydream.

I knew that face once. I'm convinced some part of me must remember even if I can't summon up mental images. A walk somewhere maybe? A dance? A kiss or more? She says a ride on a levee, and obviously there was much more. When I fell off the cliff on that day I can remember nothing about, I also fell out of this life the two of them prattle about. My heart tells me more. I was already fleeing from that life when I fell. There was a woman, Tricia by name, at the college I went to. We spoke of music and stars, and where did she fade to?

"Robert." Kelsey touches my forearm to bring my attention back to them.

"I wish I could go somewhere else for high school," John is saying. "I want to go straight to college."

"I've never seen such an impatient child," Kelsey says and pats John's arm. "I think he's upset about Henry and me." She then calls my name. "Robert. Robert, do you remember anything about us? You said you'd call the day before you went rock climbing. Especially because," and here she hesitates, sneaking a sideways look at John, swallowing, then continues in a low voice as she leans into me, "I told you I was pregnant. I thought for sure you'd call."

What called me home, again and again to Wolf Brook, where Dad said there was no future, no matter how we love you, son, don't stay here. And yet his words only made me want to come back. Temporarily, I said to myself. There was another woman, a local woman. Don't get involved here, Dad says. Move on. But there was the sweetness of acceptance and a softness of flesh of arms and legs, and after all, I had time to kill. I was between stops in my life, what was going to be my glorious life. There was a woman named Tricia. No Kelsey fits in the memories. Dad . . .

"Dad, Dad," says John, shaking me, and I look at him, startled, unable to dredge up a name, who this boy is, who insists on my attention.

"I'm sorry," I say to John, then say the same to Kelsey. "I have trouble keeping track. What do you want?"

I don't bother to sit up or swallow properly or talk slowly, so they don't catch much of what I say. I repeat: "What do you want?"

"Just listen, please, Dad," says John.

"Okay, I'll try." He wants me, my presence, disabled as it is.

Kelsey retreats from me now, sits back in her chair, looks worriedly at John and reaches for his hand. They begin an easy conversation between themselves, and Kelsey touches his arm as they speak.

"I'm sorry," I tell her. I am feeling miserable all of a sudden. I can't look at Kelsey anymore. Something about my white paper napkin offends, and I wad it up in my good hand then throw it across the room. I want to leave the restaurant, but I don't want to let her go.

"All that between us was a long time ago." She smiles and pats my hand. Her touch radiates warmth. "Except for John. He is my reminder of you." I grab her hand with my good strong right hand and I squeeze. Too hard, I realize when she frowns. But she does not pull away.

"Maybe I can make it up to you," I say. I try to maneuver my chair closer to her but my wheel gets stuck on a table leg. I tug on her hand, jerking her arm across the table, almost upsetting a sugar shaker and her cup of coffee. I give the most sincere look I can muster, one of regret and remorse and longing. "Kelsey," I say and drag my bad left hand up to grip her other arm. Now she tries to retreat. I can see fear cross her face and maybe tears welling in her eyes. With a swift tug, she frees her hand from mine.

She leans away and slides her chair back. In her face I see she is flustered, smiling nervously, brushing her hair behind her ears.

"I'm sorry," I mutter, miserable with my mistake, my lack of control. She doesn't understand what I'm saying. She smiles condescendingly and nods her head, looks to John, then at a clock behind him.

"Time to get you back home," she says, and I feel truly sad. I apologize once more and this time she understands and dismisses my words with a gesture of her hand. She lays money on the table, taking care of the bill. She and John rise and push me out of the restaurant.

In the car on the way back to the ranch, I push away from her, into the car door, wishing to melt into the vinyl and plastic. I'm trying to grasp at images, broken memories, trying to piece together a little bit of meaning. Images do come back. I remember fragments of a winter carnival, of an icy levee, of letters and long distance phone calls, and a summer when loving was easier found than it is now. I shrink as far down into my seat as I can, my eyes still able to gaze out the bottom part of my window, catching glimpses of the land, the dusty roads and pale green sagebrush of my home. Did I love her back then? And I wonder why it's important for me to know, after all this time, all these changes. By the time we get back to the ranch house, John is asleep in the backseat and has to be awakened to get me out.

"I apologize," Kelsey says as she watches John transfer me to my wheelchair, "for waiting so long to see you. I feel awful not coming sooner. Henry never liked me talking about you. You can understand that. Someday, I'll visit in Missoula with John. I promise."

I've heard such promises from folks before, but this one matters more than it should. I try not to think she will probably never visit. And that I don't deserve her to come.

26

My mom comes to the car and convinces John and Kelsey to stay and eat strawberry rhubarb pie. I retreat to my room with my tape recorder and try to faithfully preserve the afternoon while self-accusations hurl through my mind. When recalling my lunch with Kelsey and John, I think I am incredibly stupid, but my brain is unable to hold course and ferret out the import of my actions. I know there is something I need to pay attention to.

A time ago in that life my mother calls real, I was here in this house and town but didn't want to stay, yet I got involved with this local girl. She loved me; she was having my child, but all I wanted was respite before I launched into a different life. A way to kill time. Did I love her? Did I realize what I had done, conceiving a child with her?

Cyrus knocks on the door and comes in, but I am ashamed and depressed and don't want to see him. I interrupt when he starts to speak, and I rapidly fire words at him, telling him I want out of Wolf Brook, back to Missoula, on the next train. I speak too fast, and as always, he doesn't seem to care what I say. He has his own agenda and is not patient enough to wait for mine to be known.

"Let's take a ride," he says. "Around the ranch."

I don't want to go, but he's not really asking me. He assumes his plans for me are what I want, that I am unable to decide for myself. He gets behind me, and I allow myself to be pushed out of my room, outside, down the ramp to his waiting pickup. He doesn't allow me

to step and pivot, to transfer myself as much as possible to the truck seat (which is after all too high for me to transfer to without help). He lifts me, not bending properly, not using the techniques therapists teach caregivers. He stumbles with me, and I slip through his arms to the ground, hitting my hip on the running board of the truck. His face is all worry as he stands over me, and I try to reassure him. I am used to spills, and though my hip is probably bruised, this is no worse than many things I've done to myself.

I swallow and speak with as much clarity and dignity as I can muster in my awkward position, sitting in the dust by the tires of his pickup: "I don't want to go. Please help me back into my chair."

Sheepishly, Cyrus brings the wheelchair next to me, properly sets the brakes, bends with his knees, helps to lift me, allowing me to bear some weight on my good leg so I can pivot and transfer with a minimum of bounce into my chair. A few stones from the driveway stick under me. As best I can, I pull them out. I feel one buried under my thigh, too deep inside my sweat pants pocket to reach.

"I'm sorry," Cyrus says. He sits on the porch steps and removes his baseball cap to wipe the sweat from his brow. He returns the cap, places a pinch of chew into his mouth and offers me some, then quickly retracts the offer. Which is good. Because I would have taken the tobacco, would have choked on it, would have created a mess of brown drool down my chin and shirt.

"Mom and Dad are getting older," Cyrus says, looking serious. "I guess I need to take more responsibility for you. Me and Emmy." He continues, occasionally asking me questions without waiting for answers, without looking at my face. Cyrus never sees past the wheelchair. I believe he has me in mind as two conflicting images that never merge: the teenaged cocky boy, nervy to dream he is too good for here, for family, for a brother who loves the ranch and cattle and the harsh wind—and the present me, the one he pities as he pushes around, the burden he fears he will inherit once Mom and Dad are no longer able, the cripple who slurs his speech into unintelligibility, the retarded brother who's best left in another part of the state, who's got no use on a ranch anyway. Cyrus has a lot of heart, just not a lot of patience or understanding, and I have never been able to break his misperceptions. Each sentence I speak, garbled as it is, reinforces his image of me.

"Do you like living in that group home?" he asks. "I can't imagine what it's like. Mom says they're talking about you getting a place of your own. How can you manage that? They must still give you a lot of help." He pauses to spit and study his beefy rough hands. There's a lot of power in him. "Do you ever think about living here again?" he asks, and I wonder what answer he would want, if he gave me time to answer. "You never liked it here," he says. "Not much for a person like you here. Certainly not on a ranch." He wipes his forehead with a sleeve. The temperature's rising. It's hot on the plains today.

I don't try to talk. I see the house needs paint and the ramp has a few weathered boards that need replaced, and above us all, the large cloudless blue sky without trees or mountains to interrupt. I don't want to be here, I think to myself. I don't fit in this wide of an expanse. I need the boundaries of mountains, the aid of experienced people, the pavement and activity of city streets.

Cyrus, I want to shout, and maybe I do say something. I don't remember, and I know nothing I would say would make him stop talking. He is a brother examining his duty, for his sake, not mine. We had our youth together, and I know there is some love between us. I would, I think, crash through his boundaries if I could speak well and if I could maintain the focus required for a long-term siege of his resistances. But maybe I would not. Experts say the premorbid personality stays with a person after they are brain-injured, with the faults and positive traits exaggerated. Maybe the distance I feel from him and from others here at home would exist even if I were able-bodied and of sounder mind. Maybe Cyrus and I would be brothers who meet occasionally at family functions or belly up to a bar, drinking our boilermakers, telling our lies. No thinking or caring about in-depth connections. Why do I feel an attraction to that kind of life, one without intimacy?

Cyrus, I want to shout, but know it would do no good. Perhaps we both prefer the distance. I wheel away, even as he continues to talk. I look to the west where I want to return, to Transitions, to Lorna and the other folks I live with, to the caregivers who have become my life. I shift my weight and the small stone in my pocket grinds into my hip as though it's a boulder.

I think of Lorna, who could be, for all I know, dead by now, since I have been vacationing on the plains. What does she need, I wonder, that I haven't given, what needs I haven't even begun to contemplate? It's much too hard a topic, too abstract and too far away for me to handle now, and I'm told by experts we brain-injured are self-centered. We lack empathy. But you see, a small light of cognition continues to flicker inside me. At times it blazes, though briefly. I'll try to get this out before I lose focus:

I used Kelsey, then forgot her so totally I can't forgive myself. I thought I was too good for her and too good for my own family and home. I left to climb mountains, and I can't remember what other plans I had other than to get away. I ran, and she says I left a child planted in her womb. What was I thinking then when I climbed? If there are any moments I could restore to memory, it is those I would choose, when I put hand over hand, foot into crack on the side of that mountain. Was I still running from Kelsey and her child? Was I contemplating a return? Taking any responsibility? God, I feel so much pain bursting inside my head, a regret, a wish to live things over again.

I'm older now, and injury or not, I should have grown a little wiser. But I feel I haven't. I am still an object. I am being used and I use others.

I recall images of Missoula. Staff leave at the end of their shifts, present only when paid to be. The loneliness of the disabled: to be objects, to be burdens, to be jobs, to be something less than people. Perhaps it is the loneliness of the able as well, though they may not sense it as acutely. They may not know what they are missing by keeping their clients at a professional distance. But they are staff, and they are forbidden to be anything else to me. And how much do I care about their families, their homes, their wearinesses? Transfer me. Dress me. Feed me. Take me to the bathroom. And I am satisfied. Though it seems to me now, we miss such opportunities in this arrangement.

"Do you want to go in?" Cyrus says gruffly, interrupting my thoughts. I think he has been talking to me all along. "It's damn hot. I'll take you in."

"No, I want to sit out here by myself for a while," I say. But he comes around, grabs my chair and begins to push. I reach down and lock my brakes, and then he holds my hands away to unlock them. He wheels me into the house past John and Kelsey in the midst of their pie and milk. Cyrus wheels me to my room and leaves me to look out the west window, wishing I was on my way home again.

There is a soft knock on the door, and John enters quietly. From the dresser top, he picks up an old baseball trophy from a time long ago, studies it, sets it back down, then sits on my childhood bed.

"You know," he begins cautiously, "last night when you played the piano, I thought you did pretty good."

"Don't patronize me," I say. I won't accept it from my teenaged son.

"Okay," John says. "It was pretty awful." He sneaks a sideways look at me, sheepishly, unsure of my reaction.

I laugh. "Damn right," I say, "but believe it or not, I've been worse."

John laughs with me, checks himself, then says, "I'm sorry about how hurt you are."

"Be quiet," I say. "Nothing to be sorry for."

"Thanks for going to lunch with me and Mom. I can't remember you two ever being together. Even just talking with each other. Though she asks about you."

"I don't remember either," I say, "but that's no surprise."

"Do you remember anything about her?"

It seems important to him, but I can't bring myself to lie, not at this moment. "I don't remember much."

"Why?" he asks. "I thought you remembered stuff from before you were hurt."

"I don't remember too well things that happened just before I was injured. They weren't in my memory long enough. I don't think your mother and I were together that long."

"Long enough," John says.

"I'm sorry."

"She says she'd like to see you again. You don't mind if she visits, do you?"

"Whatever she wants." I'm too tired to contradict him, to tell him people are forever promising me visits that never materialize, and he speaks with such earnestness. I ask him to leave me then. I need to record my thoughts, memories of the afternoon, before I lose them, but he lingers, looking at my stuff from what was a different lifetime.

“I’ve been in here before,” he says. “When you’re not around. You did a lot of stuff.” He inspects my books, my framed diplomas, my trophies.

“I didn’t do anything,” I say. “It was a normal childhood.” I flinch at the word, normal, and he looks at me quizzically, apparently not satisfied with my answer.

“Mom says you were really smart and you played the piano and climbed mountains and could have done anything you wanted.”

I am taken aback. I wonder, what does he want? What role is he asking me to play? Is he searching for proof his father, though now an embarrassing cripple, was once a capable man, someone to be proud of back then, in his “real life”? I won’t play that game. Who gives a damn what I used to be when I am so clearly not that now?

He stares at me and I feel on display again. I’m also very tired. If I was in the group home, I could just tell staff to help me get ready for bed or to leave me alone. I could easily shut myself away, since in Missoula, they are all paid to care for me, to keep me happy. I don’t have to put up with these challenges.

“Go to hell,” I yell. “Go to hell.” His face changes expression as I see him first try to decipher my speech, and then the meaning sifting through, coming clear. “Go to hell,” I say much more quietly, more in defeat than in anger.

“Okay, I’ll leave,” John says and stands. He reaches for the door.

I don’t know why I want him to leave. In the group home, I would slam the door behind the staff as I kicked them out of my room, but now, here, I’m incapable of any action. I want to let him go; I want to be alone to sulk and contemplate, but something in his tone, in the way he holds his body, demands further response from me, so reluctantly I struggle for words that seem even harder than usual to come by. John hears me stutter, and I move toward him. He waits impatiently, uncomfortably, his hand on the doorknob, ready to leave.

“What can I do for you? What do you want?” I say finally, wondering why I want so much for the words to be the right ones.

John’s shoulders slump; he lets his hand slide off the doorknob. He stares again at me with such intensity that I have to look away. I hear him sigh. His feet shuffle on the floor. He sits again on my bed.

“I wish I could leave Wolf Brook. Now.” He only half-turns to me when he speaks.

"You got friends and family here. What's the matter with Wolf Brook?"

He gives me an incredulous teenaged arrogant stare, like how could I be so stupid. "It's just a little cow town," he says. "Everywhere smells like cow shit." He turns full on me now with his eyes glaring. "You left," he says with a finality that seems to seal the argument.

"And look what happened to me. I don't know if I'd leave again, if I had the chance to do it over."

"I don't plan to fall off no mountain."

"Okay," I say. "That wasn't in my plans either." I stop and think a minute. "Where's the guy?" I ask. "The one who was married to your mother?"

"He's gone," John says. "Found a girlfriend and left town. He was drunk a lot. Mom didn't tell you that. He was okay though."

"Do you miss him?"

"Hell no," he says and his lower lip sticks out. "He's a bastard. I just want to get out of here, for good." He's almost crying but he manages to hold back the tears.

"What's your mom think of you wanting to leave?"

"She tells me I'm too young to be thinking of it. And she wants me around, of course, now more than ever. She won't even discuss me going anywhere till I get closer to graduating high school."

"She's right. Wolf Brook's not that bad."

"Why don't you come back to live then? Instead of staying in that group home. After Transitions, maybe you'll be better enough to live out here again. You got family that would help."

"I don't know," I say, and feel my head spin. I don't want to think this hard. I can't keep up with the conversation, with his talk and ideas. He wants something from me, and I'm uncomfortable. Doesn't he know I'm the one with needs, who gets catered to? What the hell is this boy thinking?

"The last time I was in Missoula, I talked to people who work with you," he says. "They've expanded services across the state and there's people who could help you here now. It wouldn't be a group home, but you could try it here if you wanted."

"Are you saying you want me to move back to Wolf Brook?"

“No, goddamnit,” he shouts. “I just want you to understand why I want out. Like you. Like you wanted out a long time ago. And still you don’t come back.”

I breathe deep and try to relax, to put my thoughts in some kind of order, but it’s a losing battle. I quit trying to figure out what the right words are. Instead I imagine moving back to Wolf Brook permanently.

“I would miss the mountains,” I say. “I would miss my life. My real life in Missoula.”

“Okay,” says John. “I understand that.” He stands and slowly walks to the door. He turns: “If you get an apartment, maybe I could stay with you some.”

I look at him, then reach for him. He comes near, bends to put his arms around me.

A couple days later, Dad loads me into his car. He and Mom will take me back by train to Whitefish and Missoula. Emmy and a small horde of nieces and nephews gather in front of the ranch house to say good-bye. My son John gives me a hug and loops a rawhide cord over my head; it bears a clay medallion etched with a hawk, a trinket he’s made in school. The gift touches me more than I expect. I clutch it in my good hand and feel like crying. I can’t stay here, but I wish for a gift to offer John, not just some knickknack memento but some sense that I could be a father to him, give advice, be an example, whatever fathers do. I realize it is beyond me, at least for now.

“When I get an apartment, you can stay with me for a while,” I say—too quickly, so I repeat till he understands. He smiles and nods. “I will write to you,” I say and I mean it.

In the car, Dad jokes and Mom talks nonstop about what a great visit I had, how everyone loved seeing me again, how I’ll return for Christmas: maybe Cyrus will come get me. On the train, Dad leaves Mom and me in our seats as he goes to the snack car. Mom never is quiet, but there are times I love the chatter of her ways. With her voice as backdrop, I can drift into my own thoughts and think about John. I feel I have a chance to know my son, since he wants to understand me. The distance of miles may be conquered by our desires. I

don't know what I can be for him—not a father in the traditional way, but there must be something I can be beyond a crippled responsibility of his. I don't want to load too much onto a boy, but I will write him. I will write him and tell him of my life, the everyday stuff that makes up conversations and intimacies between parent and child.

27

In Whitefish, Jennifer stands on the platform, before the log chalet train station, dark jagged mountain peaks beyond, rising into a sky that, except for a few white cloud wisps, is clear and blue. She waits as I am helped from the train, her face scrunched and worried, her brunette bangs riffling in a breeze, floating now and then across her eyes. She says she hopes we don't mind but she is anxious to start the drive to Missoula.

"Crazy drivers and no speed limit," she says. "I hate driving Highway 93."

Mom and Dad are vocal with their sympathies, claiming they understand, and they seem not to mind there will be no long good-bye, despite the fact they will spend the day and night in Whitefish till the train comes back from the coast, headed east again, towards Wolf Brook.

Dad leaves to get my bags while Jennifer pushes me over wooden boardwalks to her car, and Mom walks beside us.

"Do what they tell you, Robbie," Mom says. I can't see her face, but I imagine there are tears in her eyes. She always cries at our meetings and our partings. "We'll come get you at Christmas," she promises. "I can't wait to see how much better you are." She then addresses Jennifer, "We never traveled so much till Robbie got hurt. You take care of my boy now."

I wheel away from the car, across the hard dirt parking lot, and try to orient myself by looking up, to throw caution to the wind, defy the rules and risk blindness by staring directly into the sun. I feel the sun before I see it. Instinctively—a premorbid lifetime of motherly warnings takes over—I close my eyes as my head tilts up. The warmth spreads over my face, across my chest and arms, and suddenly I feel drained. Exhausted. My head feels stale and flat. I want to get on the road.

From behind, a heavy hand lands on my shoulder, and my dad grunts something about the trip ahead for Jennifer and me. He pushes me next to the car where my good-byes with him and Mom are hurried.

"Christmas," Mom says through sighs, in her blue dress and nylons and tennis shoes. Why is she forever sad? My father is stoic, the high plains stereotype. I feel caught in his forlorn intense eyes as my car door is shut, as my window rolls down, and I feel stupidly sentimental. The etched lines of his face are deeper than I ever remember, his hair thinner, his body more frail. Years are trailing behind us. I must, I must . . . What? My thoughts falter. My mind falls painfully blank except I feel this: for him, I must do something.

He lifts one hand to wave while the other fishes out a cigarette from his shirt pocket. His mouth is crooked, one side in a smile, the other a frown. As we pull away, he turns from me. In his new stiff jeans and blue denim shirt, in his old creased cowboy boots, he walks slowly, heavily, back towards the train station.

The road stretches long in front of Jennifer and me, through the forests, the small towns, along Flathead Lake. Jennifer asks me about my trip, about my parents, about John, about the things we did. I try to tell her everything, since it feels important to communicate with her. I even tell her about Kelsey, and then she shows a lot of interest. I tell her how ashamed I am of what I have done, leaving Kelsey the way I did years ago, and then forgetting her.

After a pause in our talk, I ask, "How is Lorna?" Jennifer seems surprised by the question and makes me repeat myself.

"The same," she answers. "Not good."

"I have something for her," I say, then feel awkward. "And for you," I add and try to think quickly. I am wearing the same sweatpants as when I fell in the driveway, and the stone still lodges in the pocket, surviving washing machine and dryer. Out of my wheelchair, in the car seat, I'm able to shift around enough to retrieve the stone from my pocket, and I hand it to Jennifer. It's just a piece of gravel, not shiny or pretty. "It's from my parents' ranch. From home."

She pretends it's a better gift than it is: "Thank you, Robert. You don't need to give me anything."

"Why not? I missed you."

She laughs but then gives me a worried look.

"Everybody missed you too," she says. "It's not the same without you."

"Sometimes I wish I could be happy in Wolf Brook," I say. "With my family and my kid."

"Yeah," Jennifer says, thinking. "I'm from eastern Montana too, you know."

"I didn't know."

"From near Billings. But I could never leave the mountains to go back east," she says.

"Do you have family still there?"

"Oh yeah," she says. "My mom and a brother and a bunch of cousins. My grandparents."

"You have family in Missoula?"

"Yeah," she laughs and gives me a quizzical look. "Why all of a sudden all the questions about me?"

"Just curious. How many kids do you have?"

She laughs again, then relaxes her grip on the steering wheel, reaches for a Lifesaver from off the dash and offers me one.

"Two kids," she says. "Nine and six. A boy and a girl. What else do you want to know?"

We talk for a while. The trip feels quicker than when we came through a week before. We reach the long narrow Flathead Lake, and it's as though the water lulls us into silence, the low waves barely breaking into our consciousness. We parallel the lake a while, and I look out the window, pondering the gentle motion of the water with the breeze across it.

When we are home, I look into Lorna's room. She is not well. Though Jennifer insists Lorna is no worse than when I left, she looks much changed, nearer to total incapacitation. I am watched closely when I enter her room, and I know I will never be alone with her again. It doesn't matter. She is beyond knowing me. Death will be an appropriate release for her, I think, as I look at the tubes in and out of her. Her TV is on with the sound low. Her eyes are shut but blink open when I wheel close and hold her hand. Her breathing is heavy and strained. I think she wants to smile when she sees me though there is no movement of her lips. She whispers and I lean forward to hear. She whispers again. "Definitely," she says. "Definitely." I drop my head on my arm that is outstretched to reach hers. I don't want to let her go. I want her to rally, to return to me, to us, to the living.

"Lorna," I moan, maybe too loudly, as I hear the staff behind me shuffle feet, come closer, on guard.

I sit with her for quite a while. I don't know if staff continue with me because I never look back. I keep my eyes only on Lorna or shut them occasionally to rest them or look down at my arm, my hand, my legs. I become disconnected . . .

I imagine Lorna and me, arm in arm, walking the dusty flat gray roads around Wolf Brook. I introduce her to my family. She rests in the house while Cyrus and I ride horses around the ranch perimeter. He and I wink and joke about our wives, chew and spit tobacco, take draws on a whiskey flask, then return to the house where our wives have supper cooking. I kiss Lorna on the mouth, greedily. A couple of kids toddle into the kitchen and yank on my pant leg. I pick one of them up and lift him high above my head towards the ceiling, and he giggles and pokes at my nose with stubby fingers. In the dusk, Lorna and I stroll by the creek under the cottonwoods, sit for a while, kiss and pet, then listen to the creek's babble. We tear leaves off the tree branches, float them in the water, watch them disappear downstream, like good little dreams . . .

Finally staff pulls me away from Lorna's bed, pries my cold fingers from hers. Staff is gentle, nice, forgiving.

"Time for dinner, Robert. You can visit more later."

The next morning, case manager Jodi bustles into the group home with a rack of smiling teeth, a cheery lilt in her voice, a bounce in her walk. She greets me with enthusiasm, declaring how happy she is that I'm back.

"We have a meeting," she says breathlessly, "today at Transitions." She is perfect as always, beautiful as I remember. I don't want to look at her, but she kneels in front of me with a hand on my leg, smiling her large efficient smile.

"You look wonderful, Robert. Being with family is nice. How's your son? Pretty grown up now?"

Her words race faster than I can keep up with, and before I know it, I am shuffled into Jennifer's car and on my way to Transitions.

Everybody is there: Clare, the director; Tonya, the physical therapist; Brett; Doctor Larry; other staff; Jodi and Jennifer. Their faces are ominous, serious with traces of compassion in their eyes. I begin to feel scared.

"Glad to have you back," Clare says with a tired sigh. "We're going to use this conference today to review your progress here and give you and the group home staff recommendations for the future. Please interrupt and ask questions at any time."

I see no point in going into details. It is too painful, so I will record the highlights and leave it at that. I have failed, though no one says as much. In fact, they spend most of the time telling me how wonderful I am and what good things I've accomplished. They tell me I can continue a walking program (with walker and staff assistance). I can continue practicing to be more independent in the group home by making myself lunches, cooking with the microwave, and such. They will write all the ways I can increase my independence, and Jodi will get a copy and the group home and day service will get copies, and everybody will help me. The door to Transitions is not shut forever, they say. In the future, maybe I can come back, but for now they say I can't control myself enough, I don't show good enough judgment, to ever be safe in my own apartment. I need twenty-four-hour supervision.

Things can change, Clare says. People can change and maybe I'll get another chance later.

"Brain injuries don't change," says Doctor Larry. He's thoughtful enough he doesn't want to give false hope. Impulse control and judgment will always be difficult for me.

People change. Brain injuries don't.

Jodi pats my hand and gives me a pitying look. On my other side, Jennifer sits and rubs my back lightly.

"Sorry, Robert," Jodi says.

"Damn," I say and pound my hand on my wheelchair arm. I won't have an apartment. John won't come stay with me. "I want to keep coming here," I say, and I feel tears in my eyes. "Can't I try another week or two? One more chance? I don't want to go back to the day service. It's boring."

"I'm sorry," Jodi says.

I'm back to where I was, to what I was. My life crumples around me. Brain injuries don't change.

"Maybe in the future," Jodi says, "when we know you'll be safe."

"Can't I make up my own mind?" I say.

Jennifer says, "Isn't it up to Robert to decide what risks he wants to take? Can't he be in his own apartment knowing there could be dangers and he's willing to live with that?"

"There's liability issues," Jodi says, and then I know I've lost.

Life is too quirky. One day I am healthy and graduated from college and I have a woman who loves me. Then I fall, and for years I sit in a nursing home where no one bothers with me. I think I will die with ancient demented people all around me. Then from nowhere comes a social worker who yanks me from that and gives me new life in a group home. I am elated. I am satisfied, till again they yank at me and send me through a Transitions program and provide me visions of a more able life. Then they say it can't be.

At home, I can't bear to be with the others. I am embarrassed. I am not competent enough, the experts have declared, not smart enough. I have reached the peak of what I will be, and I have fallen too low to be retrieved. I don't yell and scream or slam doors or look to hit someone or cause any trouble. To rebel, a man needs some self-esteem.

I sit in my room and refuse dinner and company, though staff are nice and they come around regularly to check on me, to offer to sit with me if I want. One tries to lure me out with promises of brownies and card games. The pitying offers only make the pain worse.

I don't ring for assistance to get to bed, so I fall while transferring from chair to bed and always faithful staff come running at the sound. They pick me up, rearrange me, help me to get undressed and get my pajamas on. They give me maximum assist into bed, even tuck the covers around me, like I am a baby. For the first time in a very long time, I feel overwhelming waves of self-pity, and I cry because of what I am.

What I am.

I would delete this. Keep this from the final draft. Goddamn, when I started writing months ago, it was with visions of happy endings, of a glorious reentry into the real world, when I would successfully graduate from Transitions into a seminormal placement in my own apartment. And I entertained visions of John visiting me, staying for a time, maybe living with me, like people do, like sons do with their fathers. But I want no pity. Well, I do. I won't edit this. Ellen likely will argue to retain this picture of my depths, a plea to take pity on this poor cripple. But why should any of this writing be important? Why do I struggle to record my details, my feelings? What does it matter? Will anything change whether this is written or not—read or not? I am confused, lost in feeling, not sure what I want, who I am, what will happen. There is nothing here of note but the silly, stupid meanderings of self-pity, and we have all heard enough of that. Mine is no different or more important than another's. So I leave this. Know that I am miserable.

When I wake in the morning, Jennifer is in my room. She walks softly as she picks things up and speaks to me quietly about plans for the day. "It's hot out already," she says. "The weather service says we could reach a hundred today."

"Nice day to stay in bed," I say.

"You're going to day service," she says. "The Transitions PT will be there to orient staff on your walking program."

"And where will I be walking to? In circles around the hallways?"

"You'll be on your feet," Jennifer says. She brings my wheelchair and brakes it by my bed. She pulls the sheet and reaches for me. "Come on, you don't want to be late for breakfast."

I allow her to help me all she wants.

At the day service, I sit at a long brown folding table with cards dealt out in front of me, a staff and a couple of clients around me. The PT had to reschedule the walking session. From a distant corner, Jimmy yells as though he is being murdered though there is no one near him. I ignore him and the others around me, including staff. I leave the card game and wheel to the computer room where I will try to tap out this story, feeling desperate now, as though I've lost all other avenues to be heard, to be known. What ridiculous, unfounded hopes do I refuse to surrender in writing this? They are too vague and too embarrassing to put down onto paper. Ellen, I hope, will help me put all my thoughts in order.

28

Day in. Day out. I follow my routine at home, at day service. Art class, ceramics, current events. I meet with Ellen, and I faithfully record details. I refuse phone calls from my mother and try not to think of Wolf Brook, of John and Kelsey, preferring to wallow in my long deep mope.

A week passes. At the group home, Lorna weakens as hospice nurses and social workers bustle in and out. On a house call, the doctor grumbles about sending her to a hospital or a nursing home, but her family argues, and one evening, staff gather and proclaim she should die at home. There are these reminders that their service extends beyond their professional duties.

On Friday morning, Jennifer wakes me shortly before my alarm is due to buzz. She says very little but takes me to the bathroom and helps me get dressed. When we are nearly finished, she pauses, kneeling at my feet where she has assisted with my shoes, and she leans her forehead on my knee, then looks into my eyes.

"Early this morning, while we were sleeping," she says, "Lorna passed away."

At first, I am numb. I pretend I don't hear, but then a sadness creeps in that reduces me to brittleness, as though I am a glass bubble of all of life's inconsolable moments, and I will shatter with the most delicate of pinpricks. I could as easily laugh as cry.

I don't remember much afterwards. I find myself in Lorna's room where a nurse gathers wires and tubes from pieces of equipment. I remember seeing dead people before, years ago, when I was an altar boy. Lorna is like them, lying with her eyes closed, her brow smooth, her arms and abdomen free of plastic attachments, though her hair is still wet with sweat, still disheveled. I watch her chest, vainly seeking a glimpse of rising and falling. The ordeal is over, I tell myself. She is happier now, but this thought brings no comfort. I stare at her face and mumble to the nurse who can't understand me when I ask her to open Lorna's eyes one last time. I wheel forward and hold her hand, try to get closer and put an arm around her neck. If the nurse were not here, I would leave my chair and swing my body onto her bed and one last time lie next to her without tubes and medical contraptions in the way. Death has a stillness about it. Even those alive in its presence are hushed and move in slow motion. I watch her face. I swear I see a twitch, a corner of her mouth inching up. But there is just stillness.

Subdued, swift noises rise behind me. Lorna's parents are in the doorway, and they hardly notice me as I am shunted aside and they overwhelm the room. No one listens when I speak, and soon I am squeezed into a corner where I can't retreat or find a way to the door. I am witness to the family grief—restrained and dignified. Her children and her mother cry but not loudly. Her father is harried and grizzled, but I remember most the way the snaps on his cowboy shirt are off-line and crooked and how one half of his shirttail flaps outside the back of his pants. Ignored in my corner, I pray intensely that there truly is a God and a weightless heaven which Lorna can grace.

I don't remember what I do that day, if I stay home or if I go to the day service. A hospice counselor mingles among us residents, and I suppose I talk with her. Bereavement counseling.

Days pass and I perform the routines my life is so necessarily built around, though I don't lose the numb sadness. At day service, I sit at the tables, stare in front of me, and barely communicate. I ignore Jimmy and the staff and all the others. At home, after dinner, I sit in my room till the sun sets and darkness stretches through the window over me. On her downtime, Jennifer sits and worries with me, and one day as I am sitting with her, she hands me a pill and a cup of water. An antidepressant, she says, the doctor has ordered. I will take them, she says, till all this passes. I take the pill, swallow it, and she leaves. I close my eyes, hold my head in my hands and conjure an image of Lorna, a saint in heaven, healthy body, in toga and sandals, vague wings sprouting from her back. I direct a meditative prayer to her, asking for her to intercede for me, to ask God to heal me. I believe in God. I believe in miracles. Years ago, I beat the medical odds when my fate was predicted to be a long coma and death. If Lorna is a saint, can't she work a miracle or two? I obsess on the idea; I focus my meditations, strive for a vision. Gradually, I surrender to my imagination and my fantasy is this:

One afternoon at the day service, I sat at the ancient out-of-tune piano and played my Christmas songs. My prayers to Lorna had become a constant, silent chant. As I played and thought of Lorna, the fingers of my left hand seemed to grow, to stretch as they hadn't since my accident. They made the reach from middle to high C without rolling onto or banging any keys in between. I stopped my playing and studied my hand. I shook my head, chuckled to myself, and began playing again. The reach came even easier.

When I stopped playing, when I stopped examining my hands for new flexibility, Lorna's pallid face rose in my thoughts, and the absolute stillness of her open eyes terrified me.

This is, I told myself, fantasy, and I didn't tell staff about my fingers, about my improved piano-playing, though as the day progressed I noticed other subtle but significant signs that I was regaining control of my body. My foot seemed to push harder against the floor, and I was able to wheel faster. When I went to the bathroom, I didn't ask for help, and I smoothly slid onto the seat, with barely any reliance on the grab bars. I was able to lift myself just enough from the seat to pull my pants up. I transferred—again smoothly—back to the chair. As I wheeled out, I swear my mind felt less fogged, like the long cold mist was dissipating.

Yes, this was all in my imagination, but still I foraged for rationalizations that would have made this "recovery" real. Perhaps the antidepressants, I thought. Maybe a wonderful side effect was healing my brain. Or it could have been my prayers to Lorna, who was interceding for me from heaven. Or maybe I believed long enough in the possibility of a miracle that it was actually happening. My fantasy blossomed; I wanted to shout out loud, but I knew staff thought

I had poor insight and judgment. They wouldn't take any of this seriously.

At the day service, I kept myself occupied, alone at the computer, imagining strength and coordination flowing into my limbs and body. I wheeled out and found another client to play a game of Connect Four, but it was no contest as I developed a line of four red checkers quickly. I challenged a staff person, and I won easily so he asked for a rematch, taking me more seriously, and the game dragged on with each of us matching the other's move, till finally I maneuvered him into a trap and completed my row of four. I wheeled away, laughing, leaving him open-mouthed and wondering. Back in the computer room, I began to type my experiences before I forgot them, though I felt calm, no need for the usual rush to get details on paper or on tape, since I knew I would not forget as easily as usual. My fingers danced across the keys, unlike the slow banging and painful searching for keys I was used to, and my thoughts ran swift and coherently.

I would not tell staff, I promised myself, not yet. If this was fantasy—and I know well I had the ability to deceive myself—then I wasn't ready to give it up. Doctor Larry would counsel a need to face reality, but what was there for me? Lorna dead. Me kicked out of Transitions. In reality, I was going nowhere. I was not needed there. I did not want to be called back to where Lorna lay in the arid ground with nothing but her family's Mormon prayers wrapped about her. Too soon, all of our bodies would be permanently disabled in death. For a while, I would dodge reality.

After riding home in the van, I wheeled directly to my room and shut the door. My hands trembled as they locked the brakes on my chair and unbuckled my seat belt, but they were true and strong as they planted themselves on the arms of my chair and pushed my body up till I was standing. I straightened my knees, then with a sudden fearful push, I let go of the chair, and then, tottering only a little, I stood unaided. Only with the greatest self-control did I keep from calling out for a staff to witness. I took a step, right foot first, then the crippled left foot. I stayed steady though with a pronounced limp. My God, Jesus, I was walking, and then there was no way I could keep quiet. I yelled as loudly as I could. I walked to the door and opened it to meet Jennifer who had come running. She stopped dead in her tracks, her jaw dropped, her eyes wide open.

"Robert," she stammered, then grabbed for me, the amazement in her face replaced by worry. But I stepped past her and out of her reach, moving too quickly for her. "Robert," she said, "it's impossible."

"Nothing's impossible," I said, and even to my ear, I heard the difference in the way I talked. Jennifer had no need to ask me to swallow, to repeat.

If this be fantasy, I told myself, let it play out.

My recovery was considered a medical miracle. Doctors ran tests on my reflexes. They studied my hand and left foot and marveled, wondered where the spasticity and contractures had gone. They did CAT scans and MRI's, and they said somehow my brain had regenerated, had healed itself. Doctor Larry gave me a battery of neuro-psych tests. Therapists studied my walking and my stretches. Everyone's conclusion: I was back to normal, to what I was fourteen years ago before my accident.

And thus, in this, the most vivid of my fantasies, I walked outside the hospital where I had completed the latest round of testing, Jennifer beside me, the midsummer sun warming my face. Beyond the parking lot was a playground with swings and slides and monkey bars and soccer fields stretching for acres. In a far corner, teenage kids played soccer. One who reminded me of my son John dribbled the ball between three or four defenders. He feinted, he kicked. He scored. Jennifer said something, but I didn't pay attention. I dashed towards the boy who looked like John, and I was so amazed at the sensation of running I looked down at my legs, watched one foot then the other fall, hit the turf, rise again, all in a sudden blur. I was ecstatic till an image of Lorna intruded, tubes in her arms and desire in her face. Definitely. Then my feet tangled, and I tripped and tumbled to the grass. Jennifer was with me instantly, and Lorna's image faded. I lay on my back and laughed when I saw her worried face. This feels so wonderful, I told her, and raised my arms and legs and shook them to show her nothing was broken, I was whole. She laughed with me and restrained herself from stooping down, to lift me. I said nothing about Lorna haunting me, how when I looked at my feet, my eyes had blurred.

With my imagined coherence, I examined what I had written for this book. "I'm embarrassed," I told Ellen when I met with her at the day service. "It is so damned fragmented—till you edit it."

"I keep your voice as much as possible," she said.

"There's so much garbage I've written. I need to delete most of it. All the fantasies. The tangents."

"It's wonderful as it is," Ellen protested.

"You want me to make a fool of myself."

"I want you to be known."

"Wasn't I ugly enough without revealing my inner secrets?"

She stared at her hands in her lap. She spoke quietly, "I don't know how to be around you anymore. You've changed so much. I don't know what you need."

"Maybe we can be more like equals," I said. "We can kind of cowrite. Fix up this crap."

"I'd like to continue helping you," she said, "but we'll just have to see how it works out, where I fit into this process now."

We argued more about my writing and her editing. I agreed not to destroy any of it. I would continue to consult with her. Only after she made a copy did she relinquish the computer disk I had nearly filled. I slipped it into its slot and typed, thinking finally I was getting the story right, the words falling into their natural places, my thoughts organized and clearly expressed—till the letters on the screen blurred and then seemed to rearrange themselves beyond my control into a patchwork image of John. Everything—all my words and corrections—faded and disappeared then, when I hit a key accidentally. Before I could fix my mistake, I paused to stare into the blank white of the screen, blank except for the blinking black cursor at the bottom, cueing me to continue. When I looked at my fingers, hovering above the keyboard, slightly contracting, pulling into my palms, they began to ache. I tried to type more, tried to find the right key that could return me to my text, but I was frozen, unable to move. I watched the cursor, blinking incessantly, drawing my focus into it: I slid and drifted into its black flash amidst the surrounding, encompassing, serene white. I struggled in this dream state for a while, and then regained my fantasy.

Doctors continued to study me. While they did, I remained in the group home and day service. I sat at the piano which I had newly tuned, and the classical music I knew years ago returned to me. My fingers remembered the melodies, and I filled the day service building with strains of Chopin and Mozart, with a sublime beauty these walls may never before have contained. As a special treat, to make up for all the silly Christmas songs I'd inflicted on people during my years of disability, I played Handel's "Hallelujah Chorus." I lifted my eyes from the keys and saw the faces of the harried staff relax and the other clients slow down to listen. Jimmy munched on a piece of a sandwich which had been cut into small pieces for him. He slobbered and drooled, and bits of bread sprayed from his mouth when he tried to talk in his unintelligible babble. Staff tried to understand him, but he was not satisfied about something, and he yelled, then kicked out at them. The staff person backed away for a moment, then returned, joking, and asked him to listen to the music I created, and Jimmy was again content, smiling with his mouth open, showing his mashed food, drool running down the left side of his chin, his shirt a wet slobbery mess.

My hands froze above the keys. The music stopped. I should have felt empathy for Jimmy, I know. Of all people, I should have had the most understanding, but I felt nothing but disgust, and then an overwhelming shame. My God, what had normal-bodied and able-minded people thought of me? I felt an urgency to return somewhere, but I didn't know where. I remembered I had loved a woman who was like these. In the end, worse than these, yet I had lain in bed with her when she had been dying with tubes and urine bags. I became nauseous at the memories. My fingers stumbled over the piano keys, no longer able to stretch over octaves.

In and out of fantasy. I thought if I could yoke all my aspirations to my imagination, I could escape. For a while longer, I managed to do just that.

After all my doctors and professionals had finished studying me, I was put on display for others who came from around the country to see me. Jodi visited me one day in my room and told me she had arranged an interview with a vocational counselor. She thought I should continue seeing Doctor Larry to help prepare for my future. Everything had changed; I wouldn't be able to stay in the group home much longer. I'd need to decide on a job or education, a place to live. Jodi would help me for a while, though soon I would be discharged from her services.

I sat on my bed, and she sat in my recliner, close to me. I'd redecorated a bit. Replaced my Rockwell picture with a Monet of a mother and daughter walking in a field of poppies. I'd filled my shelves with classic novels and books about philosophy, and I would have liked to paint the room, change from institutional off-white to maybe a soft green or lavender. Though Jodi sat near me, she did not rest a hand on my knee like she used to. She didn't speak as sweetly or as condescendingly.

"I've been your case manager for over five years," she said. "And now you're so changed." She paused. She was not nearly as comfortable with me as before. "I don't know what to make of it," she said. "I used to wonder occasionally what my clients might be like if they were healthy, or what they were like before they got hurt. With you, I get a chance to find out." She was so serious I feared she might cry. She was beautiful in an off-white blouse with the top two buttons open to reveal a hint of cleavage. She wore her navy blue skirt and black stockings and low-heeled dark leather shoes.

"What do you think you're going to do now, Robert?"

"I want to go back to school. I don't know what to study yet, but I want to get acclimated again. Find out what I like and don't like. I'll take a few writing classes since I'm working on my book. It needs a lot of editing."

"Will you go back to Wolf Brook?"

"I'm not sure. I've talked with Kelsey a few times over the phone. She wants to see me again."

Now a worried look came over Jodi's face and she appeared more serious, even tortured.

"What will you do, Robert," she whispered and touched my knee the way she used to when I was in my wheelchair. "I've wondered often," she said, "about you, and now you are whole again, and I wonder, if before your life changes completely . . ."

She said nothing else but leaned forward, slowly and gently, so I caught a glimpse down the front of her blouse, just before her hand steadied herself on my lap and her lips came to mine: the culmination of many fantasies as she stirred and sat next to me. We fell back together into the bed, our hands and bodies searching for each other. There were no staff on guard. No boundaries. I did not have to be embarrassed by drooling kisses. Both my hands worked, open and coordinated. My fingers were straight, and they remembered what lovemaking was like before being mangled and contracted. And I noticed too there were no catheters or tubes. Nothing in our way. I left my body in place, yet I withdrew, gently, rising farther and farther away from Jodi. Her face faded, and Lorna's face intruded, with its cold stillness, its half-open eyes, staring till the nurse closed them for her.

I awoke, alone in my bed, in a sweat, remembering with a pang Lorna was dead, and Jodi remained an unreachable phantom. Then oddly—oddly because he had never been my responsibility—I wondered where my son was right then, in what bed, in what town he was sleeping tonight.

I wanted to go home to the High Line where soft arms would encompass me, keep me in a feminine lap, where lilac-perfumed fingers would caress my hair, and perfectly arched lips would whisper forever that I am complete, I am a good man, I am worthy of life, of abundant good things. Where I would be surrounded by homegrown vegetables bursting under enormous deep blue skies with faint cirrus clouds billowing in a cooling breeze and we would have Christ resurrected regularly every Sunday. Never snow, never a dry cracked earth.

That was my image of eastern Montana, that Last Best Place. If I could ever return. Truly return. Wholly. An earth-woman would wait for me, and life would be easy.

In the fantasy of my recovery, I arrived at the ranch in Wolf Brook in Cyrus's pickup on a late Sunday morning when the sun neared its highest point, and the earth wore a brown baked and cracked expression everywhere you looked. There were no clouds, just an impossibly blue sky, the color of airbrushed post cards.

I had traveled on Amtrak by myself to Wolf Brook, anxious for my family to see my new healed self, especially for John to witness his father as a whole human being again. But yet, I was afraid to see him. He alone held the power to call me back, to expose my recovery as simple fantasy. I wanted to avoid him as much as I wanted to see him.

Standing just off the porch, Mom wore a white dress, silhouetted against the blue, like some angel. She had no lines in her face, no varicose veins in her legs, no moist catch in her voice when she talked. Dad stood straight, taller than me, a strong hardened man, whose hair seemed fuller than it was in the beginning of the summer, and there seemed to be less gray. When I caught a glimpse of Emmy behind a post, I first thought it must have been one of my nieces and not my sister. She looked young, like a snapshot from my premorbid memory. My eyes, I thought, had been cleared. The head injury must have distorted my vision of these people. Cyrus put his hand at the small of my back, leading me gently towards the house, towards my family, reunited on the bright plain. We were all radiant in the sun. Cyrus leaned and whispered in my ear, "Damn glad to have you back in one piece."

Dad shook my hand vigorously, then hugged me, held me with those beefy arms and hands that had birthed calves and buried the carcasses of their mothers.

"I'll be damned," he said. "Your mother always said you'd get better, despite what the doctors predicted. Well, I'll be damned."

"Don't just stand there admiring each other," Mom said. "Let me have him. Let me have my boy. My God, look at him, standing and walking. Praise be Jesus, I can't believe it."

She stumbled back a step as I broke from Dad's grip to go to my mother, beginning with sure steps, though I felt a weakness welling in my knees as I neared her. By the time I reached her, I almost fell into her arms, and we hugged and she cried and spoke so long, so incessantly, I grew confused. My mind warped and bent and lost focus. I wanted her to be quiet, to stop going on.

"Robbie," she said, "Robbie, Robbie. It's my prayers come true. Oh, I never doubted for a moment, never a moment, you'd someday return to your real life."

This is real life, I told myself when I was given a moment alone outside where the land was flat, and brown cracked fields stretched beyond barbed wire fences to touch the sky. Two gray horses stood close by and whinnied. They stood back to front next to each other, so they could use their tails to swish the flies from each other's eyes. I was confused since seeing my mother. A feeling I couldn't identify, an uneasiness, nagged at me. Not everything was right.

From far down the driveway and the road, I saw a cloud of dust being kicked up as a car came near. I sat on the porch and smiled nervously as I waited. After the car pulled up to the house and stopped, my son John popped out and ran to me. Unlike the usual teenaged boy, he seemed unembarrassed to throw his arms around me, even to give me a kiss on the cheek. And just behind him was Kelsey. I remembered her. I knew her name. I retrieved a memory of a time shortly before I left Wolf Brook to go rock climbing, and she was there, raven-haired, and tanned brown, her eyes a penetrating green. The woman who stood before me now, who I looked at over John's shoulders as he continued to hold me, was no different from that girl of memory. She had not aged a whit. And there was a bounce in her step and a lilt in her voice.

"Robert," she said with the utmost graciousness, with a freshness that spoke of late April when the tree buds begin to blossom. I melted into the stairs where I sat, unable to move even when John rose and stood between us, his parents, and he smiled like a young child, his arms outstretched to link us.

"I hope you're here in Wolf Brook to stay awhile," she said. "John and I would love a chance to be a family with you."

I nodded, looked from Kelsey's lush green eyes to John's, that flashed like steel gray swords. His eyes had turned harsh, not approving. I stared into them, expecting to see my reflection, but I saw Lorna again, her still face looking at me from within my son's eyes. I turned away, grabbed Kelsey by the arm and walked her along a fence perimeter, walking her rapidly, leaving John behind where I couldn't see him.

That evening, I ate dinner in town with John and Kelsey at their home. I was careful to avoid his eyes, and I barely spoke with him, and I saw that he was upset, disappointed, wondering about me. After dinner, when he invited me to go to the park to play catch with a football, I tried to beg off, but I couldn't make up good enough excuses, and Kelsey urged me to go. So I found myself walking with John along railroad tracks headed for the park, while he lightly tossed the football up and down. I reminded him I hadn't passed a ball for years, but he ignored me. We would do father and son things, like normal people, as in real life. I nearly tripped and fell. I felt blinded by anxiety, to do this, to be alone with my son.

At the park, John played wide receiver while I was quarterback, and I did better than I had expected. My passes were wobbly—there were no perfect spirals—but generally they reached their mark, and John caught most of them. We played for a long time. John looked exhausted, and my arm ached, and the daylight faded. I was thrilled things were going so well, and I would not stop, would never stop, till John asked to. Our play, in fact, took on a desperation, not just that we had to make up for lost time (though that was part of it), but also I was afraid if we stopped, everything would be lost. This recovery of mine would end, would be shown to be a fraud. Much uneasiness gathered in the air under our passes.

Finally, John said, "One more pass, a long bomb." It seemed an appropriate finale. He set in a three-point stance as I leaned over the ball which lay on the ground, my knuckles over the laces. "Hike," I yelled and pulled up the ball, and John ran far into the dusky evening. He ran till I could barely see him, and I didn't pass till I heard his faint yell, then I cocked my arm and let fly—finally, the perfect spiral I had been searching for all day. The ball rose and arced, spun around its axis, then gently dropped, floated into the soft cushion John provided with his arms and body, and he never even broke stride. He lifted his arms above his head and danced like the players do on TV when they score a touchdown.

But he was disturbed when he came back, puffing, out of breath.

"Pretty nice pass," I said, ignoring the look on his face. "You didn't think your old man had it in him."

"Perfect," he said, then crumpled to the ground, lying down, still panting hard. I sat next to him.

"What's the matter?" I asked.

"Too perfect," he said and sat up. He had caught his breath. He studied me as if I were a fraud, someone who couldn't possibly be his father.

"You shouldn't stay here," he said. "In Wolf Brook. Remember, you don't like it here. You don't fit here."

“But John, everything’s changed. I’m going to find out what I like and don’t like all over again. We can be a family. Don’t you want that?”

“I want out of Wolf Brook,” he said. “Just because you’re here and you’re healthy doesn’t change that.”

“Well, maybe we all could move. Me and you and your mother . . .”

“No,” he screamed and stood and stepped away. I couldn’t see his face clearly, and it was not just because of the dusk. Something in my eyes was clouding my vision. “I need you,” he said, “the way you are.”

“What are you talking about, John?”

“This isn’t right. You don’t belong here.” He kicked at the ground with a worn sneaker. “I need you in your real life.”

“You mean being disabled? Is that what you want?”

He never answered. I didn’t quite see him walk from me, and it wasn’t so much he faded away but that everything disintegrated: the football, the railroad tracks, the field, the stars, the evening, John. Something like going blind. I yelled into the darkness.

There is such stillness.

When I empty my mind of everything, when all images are dispersed except that of the very middle of an empty white sheet, I lose myself in a deep meditation, where nothing but my pure essence exists. I have done this, you know. I am some mystic hermit, some saint who can find God in this way. But my prayers always end in a tumbling down. I never feel the ascension, only descent. I am always falling. Images intrude on my blank white sheet of collapsing buildings, of the legs of a deer buckling suddenly as it is shot, of eyelids slowly, slowly closing.

If I were blessed with an able life what mundane wonders would I replicate? Football and family and an affair for spice in small town Montana? Is this what I pine for? Perhaps it is good there are no Second Comings.

So my long fantasy ends. And it is my son John who calls me back to reality. To failure and Lorna’s death and to my still-crippled body. “Goddamn,” I yell out from my bed into the dark, raising myself on a cocked elbow. "I want the fuck out of here." I'll show staff what inappropriate can be. I kick my legs free of sheets and blankets, then try to swing them off the bed. Just as staff arrives, I tumble off the bed to the floor, bumping my head, scraping my elbow, alive with the indignity of being half-naked, bloody and hurting, spread-eagled on the floor. When the staff person reaches to help, I yank her arm and pull her down hard, causing her to trip over me, to bounce against the bed, to hit her head on a wooden bedpost. I can't help but laugh, though she has only tried to help me.

I crawl from her to my wheelchair which I try to scramble into, but the brakes aren't locked and the chair skitters away, and I fall again. My chin hits the floor, and I am bleeding. Staff grabs me from behind, trying to get her arms around me. She speaks soothingly, calmly. Inappropriate, I think, to talk so nicely in this situation. She ought to be angry. And I fling my arms back, knocking her over and away from me. I look behind and I am happy to see that finally she is mad. She is red in the face, almost crying. She grits her teeth and says nothing as she gets up and walks past, leaving me on the floor.

There will be hell to pay, I know. As I sit, I hear staff in another room pushing buttons on a phone, dialing for help.

As a disabled person I have spent a lifetime being cared for, and all relationships have been defined by assessments of my functions, of how well I perform my activities of daily living. There I am on forms in black and white with no gray, no other colors, and whether or not you are in my life or what you do in my life all depends on those forms that list my abilities and inabilities. Neither you nor I are allowed outside the boxes. Even my family reduces me to my needs, to what they can do for me. When I can focus well enough, I wail inside myself about how I am objectified, how I am defined by my boundaries.

Though it works both ways, you know. You too are bound by my functional assessments. I judge you by what you can do for me. And for this I am heartily sorry.

I envision my son above me, sitting in my chair in the corner of my room. If I try very hard, I can capture images of John as a baby laid in my lap, squawking and wriggling and kicking. His grandmother hovers close, arms ready to take over since mine are too damaged to hold on tight. These memories are reconstructions of a scene from a photograph I have studied over and over in my room when no one is around. It has been how I know my son. But in recent months, he and I have talked. His image has been lifted from sterile Kodak paper to infuse me. It is even possible he needs something of me.

I imagine John now, in my corner chair, smiling at me, telling me whatever else I am, I am not ever inappropriate.

29

I have written a poem for Jennifer, my most consistent caregiver, and maybe it is for all my caregivers:

There
in the dappled shallow pool
that tiny minnow carries spots on his back
candy apple red like the bear claw scars
on giant ponderosas reflected in the water
in the fall when sap runs
and the sugar maples turn purple.

I think I see you
there.

You see, there have been more mornings than I will ever be able to count, identical to this one, when I wake in my room and ring for assistance. Jennifer comes, as faithful and efficient as always. She braces her feet on the floor. She places one hand behind my back, rests one hand on my lap, and she helps me sit up. With her supporting my back, I swing my good right leg over the bedside. My left leg only half-follows so Jennifer reaches and guides it to join the right, both now dangling over the side. While I sit upright, safely balanced, I lift my right arm fully, my left about halfway up, and she tugs up the bottom of my pajama top, then yanks it over my head. For a moment, I am bare-chested, but she hands me a pullover short-sleeved shirt, and I am able with no assistance, though with some difficulty, to slip it over my head and fit my right arm through. She holds the left sleeve out for my bad arm so it too finds its place. She then pulls me up to my unsteady feet and supports me with her arms around me as I work my pajama bottoms off my butt. I sit back down, my private parts exposed, as she slips the pajamas off my legs. She pulls my boxer underwear over my feet and ankles, till I can reach them and maneuver them up to my thighs. I stand again, lean into her arms, and pull the underwear over my bottom. It is roughly the same procedure with my sweatpants. Then Jennifer stretches white socks over my feet and fits velcroed tennis shoes onto me. She retrieves my wheelchair and locks the brakes, then stands with her hands and arms strategically placed on me as I get up, held by her, and I pivot so my bottom is aligned with the chair seat. I flop down hard into the seat, which groans with the sudden weight but nevertheless remains steady.

I am ready for another day.

As Jennifer turns to leave, I speak to her.

"Please sit up straight," she says. "Swallow so I can understand you."

I do as she asks and repeat myself: "Thank you."

"No problem," she says. She nods and brushes a wisp of hair from her eyes and her mouth.

"I think I'm a big problem."

"Nothing we can't manage." She smiles.

"You've been good to me."

She pauses by my door where I have put up a poster of a bottlenosed dolphin floating in a slight arc just above blue water. She stares at me for a long while. Then her face grows sad.

"I haven't done anything special. I wish things had worked out better for you."

"You fought for me at Transitions," I say. "And you watched over me after Lorna died."

"It's my job."

I want to protest, to scream it's more, that people in assembly lines have jobs, carpenters have jobs, money-makers on Wall Street have jobs, but hers is an intimate service. I acknowledge that she would not be here if she were not paid, but still there are connections beyond what normally comes with a paycheck. Whether she—or I—like it, we have shared intimate moments. We are bound in some odd dance, Jennifer and I, my caregivers and I. And I know for the next thirty years, for the next forty years, for the rest of my life, this parade of caregivers will come—male and female, old and young. All colors, sizes, shapes. Whether it be in a group home, an apartment, a day service, they will dress me, undress me, take me to the bathroom, praise my moments of progress and discourage my moments of inappropriateness. At times, I will rage against their ever-presence, while other times I will plead for their help and understanding. When they are too much inside my boundaries, I will escape into fantasies where I am not disabled, where my mind and body function normally, or into fantasies where it doesn't matter that I am what I am. I can be known and loved just like any one of you. I cannot choose otherwise. This is my real life.

"You do your job well," I tell Jennifer.

"You're sweet, Robert." Before she leaves, she uses a wooden shim to prop my door open, a small kindness to make my exit easier.

Cyrus has business in western Montana, and he brings John with him, driving across the state in his pickup. The summer is ending, and this will be John's last chance to visit before school starts, when winter comes and snow will, as they say, fly. John and Cyrus arrive late, just as the dark settles.

Cyrus finds a motel, but John has been given permission to stay overnight in my room, and he lies in a sleeping bag on an air mattress on my floor. It doesn't match my visions of him staying with me in his own bedroom in an apartment of my own, but it's something. It's worth writing about.

"Are things any better in Wolf Brook?" I ask him.

"Things are the same," he says wearily. His voice cracks awkwardly, adolescently. "Always the same."

He lifts himself on an elbow to face me, his hair a tangle, his eyes bleary.

"Well, there's been some changes," he says. "Mom's dating some guy from the feed lot, and . . ." He hesitates and smiles, adds sheepishly, "I met this girl."

A part of me wants to scream: Get away! Don't be trapped. But I relax. He is young. More: he is not me.

"I don't want to stay in Wolf Brook forever," he says, his voice trailing off. He falls asleep, and I listen to his heavy breathing, the rhythms of his breaths, interrupted occasionally with a low snore, but mostly he rests easily, barely moving or turning, and I don't know why I can't sleep, why I lie still and stare at the boy on my floor. It is the first time since—since maybe in the nursing home—when anyone has slept in the same room with me.

I don't know if I move or make some sound, but something wakes him, and he sits up abruptly, and though I lie back flat and try to act as though I am asleep, pretending I haven't been watching him, he speaks to me as though he knows I am awake. He tells me all about his girlfriend—details I will never remember. He tells me about his soccer team and how when he's alone, he climbs birch trees. He talks of what seems like a hundred other things that cannot possibly be of enough importance to speak about in the middle of the night. But his words are like notes of an ancient ballad that tumble around me. I do not think he will be greatly insulted that I fall asleep with his words in my ears.

The next morning at the day service, John is still with me, though Cyrus and he will leave soon. I sit at the piano and bang away, thinking for the life of me maybe this time I'll manage to make some tune at least recognizable. John sits in a chair not far away, next to Jimmy who is telling him something about the President. I glance back to give John a sympathetic look, and I pause in my playing long enough to tell him he doesn't have to listen to Jimmy.

"It's all right," John says and waves at me, and laughs as though he's enjoying himself, as if he and I share some inside joke. I don't quite follow his meaning, but I look into his eyes, and they appear comfortable and promising.

"Keep playing, Dad," he says.

I play "O Holy Night." I don't know what it sounds like to John or staff or other clients in the day service, and I don't care. My fingers piece together parts of the melody. My brain remembers some words:

Fall on your knees;
O hear the angels' voices . . .

My fingers still can't stretch across octaves. They stumble over the keys, entwine and roll over each other, yet I play on, my son listening, my song rising:

Long lay the world
in sin and error
pining . . .

Author's Note

I first met Dan Lavelle in 1990. I was a social worker for the Montana Medicaid Division of Senior and Long-term Care, charged with monitoring, on a twice-a-year basis, the elderly and people with disabilities who received intensive home health care. Dan was my age—thirty-three—and had suffered a brain injury in a car accident in 1976. He lived in a group home and attended a day service with other adults with disabilities, most of whom had severe brain injuries. Initially, the group home and day service were frightening places to me; I had no experience with the disabled. Here were gathered individuals who could not take care of themselves due to cognitive deficits, and who weren't safe living alone. Many used wheelchairs; many, like Dan, could not speak clearly, and their speech, when it was interpreted for me by staff persons, was often tangential and non-linear, influenced by disjointed fantasies. I felt great pity but took little interest in these people I considered "retarded."

Dan had very dark hair and a bushy Fu Manchu mustache. His glasses were battered and taped, his shirt stained with food. His eyes, though not always working in sync, expressed a vague passion, and he was the most polite person I had ever met. I liked Dan, despite—or perhaps because—he was always in trouble with staff. Despite his politeness, he was not a compliant individual. But I knew nothing of him, of what lay behind the garbled speech and the injured body.

Then one day at a conference, Dan and another brain-injured man read their poetry. They read and we professional types listened, though without comprehension. Their writing teacher then translated for us, and as the words fell around me, I was stunned—and ashamed. Their words held such intelligence and feeling, while speaking of their hurts and their epiphanic joys. Here were people of profundity and depth behind their physical and cognitive injuries.

I became friends with Dan, who remains a great undiscovered poet. I found his unsullied humanity evident once I listened without a prejudiced ear. I also researched the literature on brain injury, which told me that people with brain injuries often have trouble expressing themselves the way we "normal" people do. Their speech may be affected, their physical ability to write may be lost, their thoughts may run wild, and their internal censors may be damaged. But their intelligence and emotions remain. Poetry was one of Dan's best ways to reveal himself.

Through my relationship with Dan and others, I learned that people with disabilities are not so different from the rest of us. Dan struggles every day for the routines that enable him to find the common bonds that allow communication and sharing and intimacy with those in his life.

But then, so do we all.

Tim Laskowski
Missoula, Montana
2002

Photo by Matthew Richard Holmes

The grandson of Polish immigrants, TIM LASKOWSKI grew up in Erie, Pennsylvania, earning his B.A. in social work from Gannon University. He received his M.A. in English and M.F.A. in creative writing from the University of Montana and his Ph.D. from Ohio University. He has worked in a Christian peace center, done volunteer social service work in Ireland, and worked in Child Protective Services. His fiction, poetry, essays, and reviews have appeared in many literary venues. He is coauthor of *A Race to Nowhere: An Arms Race Primer for Catholics*. The father of a teenage son, Evan, Laskowski lives in Missoula, Montana, where he is a case manager for physically disabled people.